SEARCHING FOR SUPER

MARION JENSEN

HARPER
An Imprint of HarperCollinsPublishers

ISBN 978-0-06-220958-0 (trade bdg.)

Typography by Laura Lyn DiSiena

14 15 16 17 18   CG/RRDH   10 9 8 7 6 5 4 3 2 1

❖

First Edition

For my boys

1.

VERY FINE SCREAMING, SON

The only good thing about hanging like a sleeping baby—strapped to your father's belly in an oversized canvas carrier—is that he can't see it when you roll your eyes.

But let me back up.

Dad and I hovered over a lake. It was almost midnight and the Milky Way spread across the sky like sparkling morning mist.

"Uh . . ." Dad's voice came from behind me. My arms and legs hung down in front of me like . . . well, like a sleeping baby's. "You don't by any chance know where we are, do you, Rafter?"

That isn't what made me want to roll my eyes. Dad getting lost wasn't anything new.

Usually when Dad and I go flying, he picks me up and leaps into the air. I'm thirteen and not exactly a lightweight, but he has a supersuit that gives him extra strength. And flying is his superpower. Or rather, *was* his superpower.

Tonight, it wasn't his power that kept us hovering over the lake. It was a military-grade jetpack strapped to his back. He needed one hand to work the controls, and the other to hold his phone so he could use the map application.

That's why I was in the oversized canvas baby carrier.

"Sorry, Dad, I have no idea where we are," I replied. "I wasn't paying attention."

A cluster of lights poked through the darkness on the far side of the lake, but not enough to be the city of Three Forks, our destination. Actually, I didn't think Three Forks even had a lake.

"Well, drat," Dad said. "This map application seems to be broken. Also, everything is in French."

This still wasn't when I rolled my eyes.

My dad is amazing. He's a superhero. He's also the only person I know who can get lost carrying a GPS-enabled super-smartphone.

Dad put the phone in a pocket of his supersuit. I should have brought my phone but I didn't have any pockets. I still didn't have a supersuit of my own. I was wearing black sweatpants and a black long-sleeved shirt.

Dad punched the small screen on his supersuit. The

jetpack whined louder and we started moving.

I found the North Star off to the right, which meant we were heading west. That was at least the right general direction.

The breeze against my face carried a hint of warmth. Summer lurked around the corner, and the air up here was clear and fresh. I filled my lungs with the sweetness. It felt good to be outside. Really good. I'd spent too much time indoors the past few months, doing something my Dad called *hunkering down.*

I'd started hating those two words. Hunkering down. They were supposed to sound active. Like maybe we were hiding in the trenches, waiting for the right time to charge. But really they were just a fancy way of saying we were hiding. Hiding from supervillains.

One in particular—October Jones.

I stretched out my hands, feeling the breeze rush between my fingers like water in a stream. I loved to fly. Usually, my younger brother, Benny, and I fought over who got to go out flying with Dad. But two weeks ago Benny had downloaded a new game to his phone called Virtual Goat Ranch. Now he spent his extra time raising virtual goats. Apparently, three of his goats were pregnant, and he wanted to be there as soon as the baby goats were born so he could give them names.

Dad picked up speed and the wind grew to a roar. It

didn't matter how many times I flew, I never grew tired of it. Whatever problems I had in my life, at two thousand feet everything looked peaceful. Up in the empty sky. Alone.

"Try not to move around so much," Dad called out. "You're throwing off my balance."

Well, not exactly alone.

"Sorry, Dad!" I shouted over the noise.

We flew for another twenty minutes or so before Dad slowed down.

"Is that a swamp down there?" he asked. "Does Three Forks have swamps? I *told* your mother we should have waited until morning."

Dad looked to his right. "Wait a minute. Is that . . . is that Mount Rushmore?"

Right there. *That* is when I rolled my eyes. But like I said, from my spot in the big baby carrier, Dad couldn't see me.

"Not unless we've traveled eight hundred miles off course, Dad."

"That does it," Dad said. "I'm calling your mother. She's going to have to look us up on the tracking system and give us directions."

Dad started unzipping zippers and opening pockets on his suit.

I had a sickening thought. "Just don't unbuckle my—"

I heard the whip of canvas passing through a metal buckle, and then the snug material around my waist went slack. I fell, tumbling through the night sky.

Not again, I thought.

Stars and lights from the ground spun in dizzying circles. Wind rushed loud in my ears, but I could hear Dad's voice calling from somewhere above. "I told you not to wiggle!"

It wasn't my wiggling that had made me fall, but I decided that now wasn't the best time to start an argument.

"Um . . . ," I yelled (and yelling "um" is harder than it sounds). "Dad, can I get a little help here?"

I spread out my arms and legs so that I stopped spinning. I estimated I had at least twenty seconds before I hit the ground.

"I can't tell where you are!" Dad's voice sounded closer this time and to the right. "It might help if you scream."

I could hear teasing in Dad's voice, but just to be safe, I screamed. I screamed for a solid five seconds until I felt Dad's arms around me.

"There you are," Dad said. "Very fine screaming, son."

"I get a lot of practice." I rolled my eyes for the second time that night.

"Hey, look there." Dad pointed. "It's Three Forks!"

Sure enough, the familiar Three Forks Sugar Beet Factory loomed off to our left, its large cement smokestacks cutting into the sky.

Dad strapped me back into the carrier and then flew down to read a street sign. He flew up, over, and back down to read another. He repeated this until I felt certain the mashed potatoes and chard I'd eaten for dinner were having a wrestling match in my belly.

Finally, we reached our destination—an old house just beyond the city limits where we were supposed to meet my cousin.

Well, I use the word *cousin* loosely. I have hundreds of relatives—maybe a thousand. Uncles, aunts, cousins, second cousins, cousins once removed. We're spread out all over. There are Baileys in every major city and township in the country. I've found it's easiest just to call everybody cousin, unless they're old. Then they're an aunt or uncle. If they're really old, or look a little insecure, I call them great-aunt or great-uncle.

Dad landed on the lawn. Or what had been the lawn once. Now it was mostly weeds, dead grass, and crusty dirt. Paint peeled from the small white clapboard house. Brown vines clung to the walls, as if they were trying to pull the building into the earth. Bits of trash lay scattered around the yard.

I checked the address on the side of the home. "Who are

we meeting here again?"

"John Bailey," Dad said. "And his nephew. They were the only survivors of the Joneses' attack here in Three Forks."

He took off the jetpack and leaned it against the porch. Dad climbed the stairs, then rang the doorbell. "I forget exactly how we're related. I think it's through your great-uncle Hjalmar Eugene. Or maybe it's *my* great-uncle Hjalmar Eugene. Either way, I'm sure he was great. Because he was a superhero."

I gave Dad a courtesy laugh. "How did Uncle John know to call Grandpa?"

"Probably like the rest who are calling him," Dad said. "They just keep trying different places until somebody picks up the phone."

Two months ago, we'd been attacked by a family of supervillains known as the Joneses. Benny and I, with help from our superfriend Juanita Johnson, had been able to stop them in Split Rock, but not before the villains had stolen everyone's superpowers.

I guess technically we still had superpowers, although I don't think I'd call them super. My brother could change his belly button from an innie to an outie. Dad could burp in Russian. I could strike matches on polyester, not just on matchboxes.

We weren't exactly what you'd call a threat.

And it didn't just happen to us. We'd started getting calls a few days after the attack. The Joneses had attacked superheroes everywhere. Most of our relatives had gone missing, but a few managed to escape. All of them had lost their powers, just like us. Since everybody in Split Rock was still accounted for, that became our home base. One by one, superheroes started gathering at Split Rock.

Gathering to hunker down.

Dad rang the doorbell again. Candlelight flickered inside the house. A voice called out, "Sorry, it's hard for me to get up. Let yourselves in."

Dad looked at me and raised his eyebrows. He opened the door, and we entered the house.

Things were as rundown inside as they were outside. Light from several candles bathed the room in shadows. Stacks of newspapers, magazines, and grocery sacks sat on top of every flat surface. A collection of stuffed animals rested on boxes in one corner. They seemed to stare at me with empty eyes. A dishwasher lay on its side against the far wall. A large vase containing a dead cactus perched on top.

An old man sat in the front room. Crutches lay on the floor next to him, and he had one leg propped up on a milk crate. A cast covered his leg from ankle to knee. Five toes stuck out of the white plaster like little mushrooms. He had a blanket draped across his lap and a bandage wrapped around his head that covered one eye and half his face. White whiskers poked out around his jaw and chin. He looked familiar. I must have seen him at one of our family's many reunions.

Dad walked across the room and held out his hand. "Hubert Bailey," he said. "I don't think we've met. I'm the great-grandson of Gjorts Ingavald Bailey."

The older man leaned forward and shook hands with Dad. "John Bailey," he said. "Son of Hjalmar Eugene. Sorry for not getting up. The doctor says I shouldn't put any weight on this leg for at least another week."

Uncle John sat back and motioned with his hand. "Please, have a seat. My nephew should be out in a moment."

I looked around. An old sofa sat against the wall by us, but a large stuffed moose rested on top of it. Not just a moose's head, but an entire stuffed moose. Someone had positioned a cone-shaped party hat between the moose's antlers.

"Yes, well uh . . . ," Dad said. "We're fine standing. How are things with you?" He motioned toward the cast. "Is that from the attack?"

Uncle John nodded. "I was on the roof hanging up our decorations for National Peanut Month. There was a flash of light, and suddenly I don't have my powers. I'm a Stretcher—or rather, I used to be. I'd gotten on the roof by stretching, so there I was, stuck up there without a ladder. I hit a patch of ice, and the next thing I knew I was waking up in the hospital with this." He motioned to his leg. "I got out of the hospital a day later and found my nephew, who had managed to avoid being captured. Of course we immediately assumed it was the Johnsons."

The Johnsons are another family of superheroes. For years, members of our two families had been fighting—in every major city in the country—with both families claiming to be the real superheroes. I'd thought Juanita Johnson was a villain, until she became my friend.

"But the Johnsons had gone missing just like us, and when we finally found you all up in Split Rock . . . well, you told us it wasn't the Johnsons. That's when we started looking for this third family. The Joneses."

I had been staring at all the crazy stuff in the room, but this comment focused my attention back to the conversation. "Have you found anything? About the Joneses, I mean?"

The Joneses. The real family of supervillains, they had kept the Johnsons and the Baileys fighting for decades. They'd stayed hidden in the shadows, doing who-knows-what while the superheroes fought among themselves.

Uncle John shook his head. "Haven't found a thing. It's like they don't even exist. We're still chasing down a few leads, and . . . well, my nephew and I, we're working on a few other ideas."

I was starting to like Uncle John. Only two Baileys had survived the attack here in Three Forks, but it sounded like instead of hunkering down, they were doing something. They were fighting back. In Split Rock, we had almost eighty Baileys and Johnsons gathered from all over the country, and all we'd managed to do was perfect the art of hiding.

"We've been able to piece together what happened," Dad said. "After they took away everybody's powers, the Joneses rounded everyone up and took them."

"Took them? Took them where?"

Dad shook his head. "We don't know. One Bailey from Nebraska said that no one was hurt, but he watched his family get loaded into a bus. The bus just drove away."

Uncle John rubbed the stubble on his jaw. "We've got to do something. All of these missing superheroes. Super-villains hiding and plotting, plotting and scheming." Uncle John looked me in the eye, his voice low and serious. "It's only a matter of time before everything falls apart."

I nodded. I had the sudden desire to stay in Three Forks and help.

I jumped at a noise coming from the kitchen.

"Ah, here's my nephew now," Uncle John said.

A older boy carrying a backpack entered the room. I put him at about sixteen or seventeen. His blond hair flopped over green eyes. He was muscular and tan. He looked . . . well, put him in a supersuit and he'd look exactly like a superhero.

"Hi," the boy said, crossing the room and holding out his hand. "I'm Thimon."

It took me a split second to realize that he had a lisp. "Simon," I said. "It's nice to meet you."

"It's not Simon," the boy said, smiling. "It's pronounced Thimon. My parents had a weird sense of humor."

"You mean . . ." I'd never heard of such a thing. "Your name is really Thimon? Like . . . T-H-I-M-O-N?"

Thimon nodded.

I didn't know what to say. "Sorry about that."

Thimon shrugged. "It could have been worse. If I was a girl, they were going to call me Thethily."

Dad cleared his voice. "You said on the phone that only Thimon is coming with us. Are you sure you won't come too? Split Rock is very likely the safest place in the country right now."

Uncle John shook his head. "Thimon and I were following up on a few last leads here. I'll wrap them up, let my leg heal, and then I'll make the trip. Two or three weeks. A month at the most."

Dad cleared his throat. "Well . . . It's a school night for

Rafter. We probably should get going."

He didn't seem interested in whatever Uncle John and Thimon were working on, but as soon as I got a chance, I was going to ask. I wanted in on it.

Thimon was shipping most of his luggage. We said our good-byes to Uncle John and headed out to the front lawn. Dad put on the jetpack and strapped me into the front and then wrapped his arms around Thimon.

"Ready?" Dad asked.

"Yep," Thimon said.

"Me too," I replied.

Dad pressed the controls on his wrist. The jetpack whined to life and we were off.

The wind was too loud for us to talk much. I used the time to think instead.

Hiding. Waiting. Watching.

The one time in my life when I'd felt almost super was when Benny, Juanita, and I had saved the day. We hadn't hunkered down. We'd run out into a dark night and faced a supervillain. Ours was the only city where all of the super-heroes had escaped capture, thanks to us. We'd beaten a supervillain.

We'd beaten October Jones.

October Jones is not somebody you'd want to meet in a dark alley in the middle of the night, or in a nice park in the middle of the day. Or anywhere, for that matter. I'd met him and almost hadn't survived.

The wind blew into my face, stinging my eyes.

October was a Super-super, which meant he didn't have just one power. He had *all* the powers. I still remember the last thing he said to me before getting into his helicopter and disappearing into the sky. *Now I know your name, Rafter Bailey, and believe me, that's not a good thing.*

Sometimes when the sun was shining and I was safe in my house, I could convince myself that October Jones had forgotten about me. That he'd moved on to more important things.

But other times I remembered the look in the villain's eye. The look of hatred.

October Jones didn't forget.

Hunkering down isn't what makes a hero. Heroes get up and do something. Something big. Something important. Something that everybody notices.

That is what I needed to do.

2.

I'D CONK HIM ON THE HEAD

"Pass the goat's milk, please."

I slid the jar of white, frothy liquid across the breakfast table to Benny, then realized a second too late that he wasn't paying attention.

"Heads up!"

Benny caught the goat's milk just before it fell off the edge of the table. He poured it over his rice, then sprinkled on spearmint leaves and stirred it all together. He chewed on the warm mush as he poked at his phone.

"Is Sinclair a good name for a goat?" Benny never looked up from his phone these days. "I've got twenty-six goats, and only five of them have names."

"Do you want seconds, Rafter?" Dad asked.

I shook my head. I'd eaten enough of the superhero diet for one morning. The diet only allows us Baileys to eat certain foods, none of which are bacon.

"Did you know the Johnsons don't have a superhero diet?" I asked. "Juanita was telling me that sometimes for breakfast, she eats a cereal that has *marshmallows* in it. Do you hear what I'm saying? Marshmallows for breakfast."

Benny burped. "Excuse me. Ugh, goat's milk doesn't taste as good coming up as it does going down."

"Just because the Johnsons do something doesn't mean that we should do it," Dad said. "Marshmallows for breakfast isn't going to win you any battles with a supervillain."

"Maybe not," I grumbled. "But if I got in a fight with a supervillain, I wouldn't want my last meal to be warm goat's milk and rice."

We'd gotten home late last night, and Thimon hadn't come out of his room yet. Dad said he'd finished his school year in Three Forks, so he wouldn't be attending school here.

My older brother, Rodney, came into the kitchen, still wearing his pajamas and a bathrobe. His superpower had been all in his brain. He'd graduated from high school back when he had his power, even though he was only sixteen. He'd spent the last three months struggling with our computer systems trying to get everything working again. Without his power, he was having a hard time getting the systems back online.

Rodney held a tablet computer in one hand and a tooth-brush in the other. "Hey, Dad," he said, reading from his tablet. "Did you hear about Uncle Buford over in Haver-ford?"

"Yes, I did," Dad said. "But in his defense, the lumber-jacks shouldn't have stolen his chocolate milk in the first place."

"No, not that," Rodney said. "He's missing."

Dad put his spoon down and wiped his mouth on his sleeve. "Missing? What are you talking about?"

"Aunt Ellen called Grandpa this morning," Rodney said. "Uncle Buford went out last night to do some shop-ping. He never came back."

Dad scratched his chin. "I'll admit, Buford has never been that good at shopping, but even he can't be that bad."

No one said anything until Benny finally said what we were all thinking. "Did the Joneses take him?"

"I don't know." Dad drummed his fingers on the rim of his empty bowl, and then stood. "I'll go out to the ranch after work and talk with Grandpa. Rodney, send a mes-sage to all the Baileys. Tell everybody to be on guard. Oh, and contact Mrs. Johnson as well."

Mrs. Johnson was Juanita's grandma. It was hard to believe that just a few months ago we had thought of her as our enemy. Now we were working together.

"The bus!" Benny jumped to his feet, shoveling the last of his breakfast into his mouth. "We're off!" he hollered as he raced from the room.

I got up and grabbed my backpack.

"Be careful!" Dad shouted. "Bus, school, bus, home. Don't go anywhere else. And remember—"

"We know, we know," Benny called over his shoulder. "Hunker down."

Benny and I ran to catch the bus. We took a seat toward the middle where we could speak in hushed voices and not have anyone overhear us.

Benny frowned.

"I'm tired of hunkering down," he said. "We should be out there"—he jerked his thumb toward the window—"searching for October Jones."

"Yeah?" I asked. "And what would you do if you found him?"

"I'd conk him on the head," Benny replied. "After I made him give me back my speed, of course."

"You'd conk a Super-super on the head?" I asked.

"Sure I would," Benny said. "I'm very good at conking. Besides, he might not be a Super-super anymore. You took away his powers."

This was the debate that had been occupying the Baileys and the Johnsons for months. Nobody knew if the Joneses still had their powers. I'd destroyed the device that had switched everybody's powers in Split Rock, but the Joneses had used similar devices in every major city in the world. It was easy enough to imagine that they'd simply used another one.

But if they *did* have their powers back, why didn't they just come after us? Without our real powers we'd be unable to stop them. They could take us wherever they were taking our relatives, and that would be the end.

So far, they hadn't made a move.

"I don't know, Benny," I said. "Let's see what Dad says after he talks with Grandpa."

Benny pulled out his phone. "Sweet! My goat Rafter is pregnant again. She always has at least five little goats at a time."

"You named a goat after me?" I asked. "A girl goat?"

"It's harder to come up with names than you'd think," Benny replied.

Benny played with his goats, and I watched the houses roll by outside the window. As more kids got on, the bus began to fill with conversation.

"My dad couldn't even come to my birthday party last night."

It took me a second to recognize the voice of my friend Mike. His dad was a Split Rock police officer.

"How come?"

I didn't recognize the second voice.

"Crime is getting out of control," Mike said. "The super-heroes have disappeared. Nobody knows what happened to them. I mean, they really didn't do much before—they kind of just fought each other—but I guess the bad guys knew they were there. Now my dad is gone before I wake up, and sometimes I'm already asleep by the time he gets home."

I looked over at Benny, who was still focused on his phone.

I didn't like what I was hearing. Before the superhero families started working together, I thought we'd done more harm than good. But we'd stopped going on patrols now that we were hunkering down, and if that meant crime was on the rise . . . I made a mental note to talk to Dad about it when I got home.

The bus came to a stop, and Juanita climbed on. She wore blue jeans and a red shirt. Her hair hung in dark curls around her shoulders. I waved. She smiled and waved back.

"Hey, Benny," I said. "If you're going to play on your phone, can you move forward a seat so I can sit with Juan-ita?"

Benny didn't even look up as he shuffled into the next seat. I stood to let Juanita sit by the window.

"No Monroe today?" I asked.

Monroe was Juanita's cousin in the same way Thimon was my cousin. He'd come to Split Rock with his father, and now they both lived with Juanita and her dad.

"No, he's coming." Juanita rolled her eyes. "He tripped over a sock last night and now he's claiming his ankle is sprained."

Benny poked his head over the seat. "He tripped over a sock? How does that happen? Don't you just kind of . . . step over it? Or on it?"

Juanita laughed. "Good question, Benny. I think he's just faking it so he can make my dad bring him food, and get out of doing his chores."

I looked out the window and watched as Monroe hobbled on two crutches toward the bus.

He was only seven years old. The bus dropped off a load of younger kids at a nearby elementary school. Monroe wasn't old enough to know about the Johnson family secret—that they're superheroes. But back in his hometown, he *had* noticed that Johnsons and Baileys weren't supposed to get along. He'd brought a healthy dose of *I hate all Baileys* with him to Split Rock.

For example, the first time I met Monroe, he walked up to me on the playground and bit my ankle.

Our relationship had gone downhill from there.

The bus driver jumped out of his seat to help Monroe onto the bus. Monroe paused at the top of the stairs, waved at everybody, and then said good morning in a high, squeaky voice. Monroe had dark curls and large, brown eyes. He was short for his age and had a slight gap between his two front teeth that sometimes made him whistle when he said his *S*'s. Everybody immediately fell in love with him.

He stumbled toward us, all smiles and grins until the exact moment he sat in the seat across from Benny. Suddenly, his high, squeaky, cute voice became a high, squeaky, cute growl. "Good morning, you pot lickers." He ended *lickers* with a whistle.

"Cram it, Monroe," my brother said.

"Just ignore him, Benny," I said. "You're never going to win a fight against a cute seven-year-old. You'll end up looking like a bully."

"Monroe, be nice," Juanita said.

"They're Baileys," Monroe said. "This *is* me being nice." He turned his head and made a spitting sound. Back when we were fighting, every time the Johnsons said our name, they spit. We countered by shaking our fist every time we said their name. Seeing Monroe do it made me realize how silly it was.

I heard the crinkling of paper in the seat in front of me. Sometimes Benny stayed up at night writing down insults he could hurl at Monroe. None of them were any good, and it made it worse that he had to read them.

"Monroe," Benny said, "when you were born, the doctor took one look at you and said, 'Oh my, this baby is not a pretty baby.'" Benny snorted, and leaned over the side of the seat. "Rafter, am I right?"

I shook my head. "I'd say stop while you're ahead, but I don't think you were ever ahead."

Juanita laughed, and that made me happy.

Benny went back to his paper, and started reading more insults.

"Sorry about that." Juanita smiled. "I've tried explaining to Monroe that our families get along now, but I guess the Baileys back in his old city were pretty mean."

"Couldn't you tell him about the family secret? That would clear things up."

"I asked my dad," Juanita said. "For now, I guess we have to put up with it."

It had taken a while for Juanita to really trust Benny and me, but once she did, I was delighted to discover that my arch nemesis was a very likable person. She was also smart. She could think and plan and look at a situation from every angle. This was a good contrast to Benny, who had one approach—lower his head and run toward the danger.

Juanita didn't always follow along with everything I said, and I liked that. She challenged me to see things in new ways.

She also helped me remember why we were superheroes. I loved to think about tactics, but Juanita was always thinking of others. She was a kind person. Right down to her shoes. Recently she was on a volunteer kick. In fact, it was the one exception to "hunkering down" that my parents had allowed us. We could hang out with Juanita when she'd found a new place to volunteer.

"Oh," I said, remembering. "My uncle Buford disappeared last night. He went shopping and never came back."

Juanita looked concerned. "He went missing? Have you contacted the police?"

I shook my head. "You know, now that you mention it, we haven't. You'd think that would be the first thing we'd do. Maybe my dad thinks he can handle it better than the police. He's going out to Grandpa's place to talk about what to do next."

"I'm surprised your parents let you come to school," Juanita whispered. "My dad says that if the Joneses make a move, we're all hiding at our headquarters. He thinks October will want to get revenge on the three of us more than anybody else."

Benny and Monroe were getting loud.

"Seriously, Benny, just ignore him. Go back to playing with your goats."

Monroe slid across the seat so he could see both Benny and me. "I've got two words to say to you guys." He paused, and then in his high, squeaky, dramatic voice, he said, "You two are morons."

"Monroe," Benny said, "you need to go back to kinder-garten. That's five words."

I counted in my head. "Actually, it's only four words."

"No . . ." Benny started counting on his fingers. "You . . . two . . . are . . ."

"You're counting syllables," Juanita said. "Rafter's right."

"Oh," Benny said. "Four words. But nowhere near two."

Monroe didn't stop to argue. He picked up one of his crutches and poked Benny in the ribs.

"Ow!" Benny said. "You little stinker."

I turned my back on Monroe so I could keep talking to Juanita, but as soon as I did I felt a sharp pain in my side. Monroe had started poking me.

"Monroe Johnson," Juanita said, her voice firm. "You leave them alone."

Another jab. I decided to take my own advice and ignore him.

"So, do you think the Joneses kidnapped your uncle?" Juanita whispered.

Another jab.

"I don't know," I said. "I wanted to ask you if anyone in your family had gone missing."

Another jab.

Juanita shook her head. "Not that I've heard of."

Another jab.

"Like I told you," Juanita said. "If something did happen, my dad and grandmother would probably lock me away in—"

I timed it beautifully. I spun in my seat and grabbed Monroe's crutch right as he tried to poke me. He pulled the crutch back and the rubber tip on the end popped off in my hand.

"Now please leave us alone," I said.

Monroe glared at me with cold eyes. He made a pitiful sobbing noise, and then his face went from a scowl to a perfect depiction of agony.

It seemed like the entire bus turned around to look at us. A girl sitting in the front came back to check on Monroe, who rubbed at his big brown eyes until it looked like he was going to cry. He hung his head and rocked back and forth in the seat.

The kid deserved an award for acting. Even I started feeling sorry for him.

"Monroe!" the girl said. "What's wrong? Does your foot hurt? Do you need a doctor?"

Monroe lifted his tear-streaked face. His lip quivered, and he pointed a trembling finger at me.

"That muh . . . muh . . . mean boy," Monroe said through fake sobs. "He broke my little crutch." The word *little* came out as *widdle*.

The girl turned and looked at me like she'd just discovered a cockroach in her milkshake. I knew when I'd been beaten. I tossed the rubber tip to Monroe. Unfortunately, it hit him in the forehead, and he shrieked. "He hurt me in my brain!"

"You bully!" The girl sat down next to Monroe and put a protective arm around him, as if she expected me to leap out of my seat and start beating on the little guy.

I sighed and rested my head against Benny's seat. "Outsmarted by a seven-year-old."

"It's not that bad," Juanita said.

"Oh?" I asked.

"No," she replied. "He'll be eight next month. You were outsmarted by an almost-eight-year old."

That made me laugh. I blurted out, "I'm glad we're friends, Juanita."

I felt silly as soon as I'd said it. For a moment, Juanita just looked at me. I couldn't read her face.

And then she smiled. It was a perfect smile.

"I was always a little jealous of you and Benny."

"Jealous?" I asked. "Why?"

Juanita lowered her voice. "Being super is lonely. There are things you can't talk about. Not to your friends, at least. You always had Benny, and I didn't have anybody. But now I feel like I have somebody too."

A memory jumped to my mind. Benny and I were waiting to get on the bus. It was when we thought Juanita was a Super-super and that she was out to get us. I'd been terrified. I'd wanted to run. But Benny was there with me. My brother gave me courage.

Juanita had gotten on the bus that day by herself. She'd known she wasn't a Super-super, but she'd thought she was facing two kids who were supervillains.

She'd done it by herself.

Now there were three of us. The three of us who had stood up to October Jones. Together, we were strong.

"I am your friend, Rafter Bailey. And I'm glad you're mine."

The silence suddenly became awkward. I could feel the blood pumping in my temples, and I felt my face grow red.

"Do you know what I think it means to be a friend?" Juanita asked.

I shook my head.

"Maybe it's silly . . ." Juanita's eyes held mine. "I think a real friend is always there for you. No questions asked. That's the kind of friend I am. If you or Benny ever need me, I'm there. No matter what."

Now it was Juanita's turn to get all shy. She looked down. I told a stupid joke to break the tension. She laughed, and the moment passed.

But it wasn't forgotten.

We talked all the way to school. Even when other kids filled in the seats next to us, and we couldn't talk about superhero things, we talked and laughed. The sun was bright, and school was almost over for the year. It was a beautiful day. A wonderful day.

The calm before the storm.

3

I'VE ALWAYS WANTED TO SING BASS

"Hahm mort." Benny lay facedown on his bed, his head buried in his pillow. His words were muffled, but I knew what he'd said because he'd said it six times in the last five minutes.

I'm bored.

Thimon sat on our bedroom chair, flipping through screens on a tablet. I shoved the history report I'd just finished into my bag. It was the last of my homework. Three more days and school was out for the summer.

"Why don't you read some more manuals?" I asked my brother.

Benny loved reading manuals. He'd started with the ones for the vehicles in the Bailey motor pool, hidden underground beneath Grandpa's ranch. Then he'd moved to the ones for our weapons, our tools, and even our super-suits. He was barely passing his classes at school, but he devoured anything he could get his hands on when it came to our equipment.

"Burk id drying do bind be—"

"Benny," I said. "I can't understand you. Pull your face out of your pillow and use your big-boy words."

Benny rolled onto his back. "Dirk is trying to find me another manual on the Dirt Hog. I dropped the first one in the bathtub."

The Dirt Hog is a cross between a motorcycle and a snowmobile. It has two wide tires and is made to ride almost anywhere. It's heavily armored. If it can't climb over something, it will just break right through it.

Benny sighed a happy sigh. "The Dirt Hog is the cool-est thing since . . . well, think of something really cool. It's cooler than that. But Dirk won't have the manual until later this week."

"Play with your goats," I said.

"It's wintertime in the game," Benny said. "All the goats are hibernating."

"I don't think goats hibernate."

"My goats do," Benny said. "But luckily winter is only twelve hours long."

Thimon told us his dud power gave him the ability to

go up the down escalator. Not by running fast, either—anybody could do that. The escalator itself would reverse direction as soon as Thimon stepped on it. Benny had been begging to see it ever since.

Benny sat up. "I know, let's go to the mall and check out Thimon's thuperpower."

"Superpower," I said. "Don't make fun of Thimon's name."

"I'm not," Benny said. "Thometimes . . . I mean, sometimes it just slips out."

"Don't worry about it." Thimon threw a pillow at Benny. "Although I doubt going to the mall is your dad's idea of hunkering down."

"No one's going to attack us at the mall," Benny said. "Although I wish they would. Nothing ever happens anymore. There are no villains. There are no battles. And our supersuits won't be here for another week or so. How are we supposed to be superheroes if nothing big and exciting ever happens?"

For a second, we'd thought Uncle Buford's disappearance was big and exciting, but now it was looking like maybe it wasn't. It turned out Uncle Buford was a flight attendant, and Aunt Ellen admitted that he had probably just gone to work and forgotten his phone charger.

"I can't go to the mall." Thimon continued to flip

through screens on his tablet. "I'm working on some stuff for Uncle John."

This was the opening I'd been looking for.

"Oh yeah?" I tried to sound casual. "What are you working on?"

Benny moved to the edge of the bed. We both stared at Thimon, eyes eager.

Thimon stared at us for a moment, and then set the tablet on my desk.

"Look, guys," he said. "I'd really like to tell you, but . . ."

"We can totally keep a secret, if that's what you're worried about," Benny said. "Well, unless I get tickled. But if somebody tickles me, I'll just tell them a different secret. Like the time Rafter was at this fancy dinner, only he couldn't find a restroom. He had to—"

"Benny," I said. "Now is not the time."

Thimon seemed to consider our request. "I'm sure you guys can usually keep a secret. But this is family. Families don't keep secrets very well. If I tell you, then of course you'll tell your parents. And your dad will tell his dad, and then everyone will know. Uncle John and I are working on something, but right now we can't tell anyone. Even family. Does that make sense?"

Benny looked disappointed, but nodded. I felt less certain.

Frustration built up inside of me. All of this waiting and watching. The hunkering down. Three months ago, I'd gotten a taste of what it felt like to be super. I'd done something big and important. For one brief moment in time, I'd been almost super.

I wanted to finish the job. I wanted my real power back, and I wanted to beat October Jones. Nobody was doing anything except for Thimon and Uncle John.

I made a decision.

"What if we promise not to tell anybody. Even our parents?"

Thimon shook his head. "No, I couldn't ask you to do that. That wouldn't be right."

"It wouldn't be right for you to ask us," I said. "But you're not. I'm offering it. If you tell us, we won't tell anybody, even our parents. Right, Benny?"

Benny looked from Thimon to me. Benny could never hide his feelings. I saw the struggle playing out in his head. He gazed at me for what felt like a long while, then he said, "If you think it's okay, then I won't tell anybody."

Thimon looked from Benny to me. "Okay. As soon as it's possible, we can tell the rest of the family. You won't have to keep this secret for long. But for now, it is important that nobody else knows. Promise?"

Benny and I both promised.

Thimon got down from his chair and sat cross-legged

on the carpet. He leaned against the wall, and Benny and I joined him on the floor to listen. Thimon's face became serious. It felt like we were having a war council.

"I didn't tell you the truth about my power," Thimon said. "I can't actually do anything to or even around escalators."

"Aw, man," Benny said. "I won't lie. I'm disappointed."

"I used to be a Shrink," Thimon continued.

"We had one of those," Benny said. "Great-uncle Pete over in Oak City. He could shrink to roughly the size of a chimichanga."

Thimon nodded. "I lost my real power, just like everybody else. But instead of getting a dud power . . . I got something better."

I caught my breath.

Benny leaned forward, his face eager. "What did you get?"

Thimon crossed his arms. "I was with some friends outside of town when we all got dud powers. I was delayed in getting back into town."

"That's not a power," Benny said. "That sounds like a story."

Thimon laughed and continued. "My family thought the Johnsons were behind it and when they got word the Johnsons were gathering at the fairgrounds, they decided to go battle them—try to get back their powers."

"But instead it was the Joneses who were there waiting for you, right?" I asked. "They tried the same thing here. They were trying to trap us."

Thimon nodded. "But like I said, I was delayed. By the time I got to the fairgrounds, it was clear what had happened. I watched as all of the superheroes—both Johnsons and Baileys—were captured by the Joneses, and loaded onto buses."

Thimon's head was down. He pulled at strands of the carpet. He didn't say anything for a few seconds. Finally, he cleared his throat. "I didn't do anything to stop it."

"You couldn't have done anything," I said. "If you'd tried, you wouldn't be here. You wouldn't be in a position to help them. It was the right choice."

Thimon looked at me like he wanted to believe me, but still wasn't convinced. This is why he was fighting back, I realized. He was doing this because he felt like he had failed his family.

"That's a great story," Benny finally said. "I really like the part where you finished it. Now can you tell us your real power?" I could see that Benny was about three seconds from reaching out and shaking Thimon by the shoulders.

Thimon leaned forward and lowered his voice. "I can temporarily grant someone else a superpower. I can make anybody super."

I didn't know what to say. Partly because I didn't

understand what Thimon meant. Benny must have felt the same way. It seemed too good to be true.

My brother recovered first. He leaned forward, knuckles on the carpet, until he was almost nose to nose with Thimon. "Do you mean to tell me that you can give me my real power? Speed? Right now, you could give me super-speed?"

Benny's excitement was contagious. Thimon grinned and nodded. "I have seven powers I can give you."

"That's like making us a Thuper-thuper!" Benny said. "Sorry, I mean—"

"Not quite," Thimon said. "I can only give you one at a time."

"Thimon," I said. "Could you give all of us power? The entire family? If we had a hundred Johnsons and Baileys with superpowers, we could—"

"No," Thimon interrupted. "It takes a lot of effort to give even one person a power. If I really concentrated, I *think* I could give two people powers, but that's it. I can't even give powers to myself because it takes so much concentration."

Real powers. I remembered what it had felt like when I had my power—strength. I'd had it for only a few minutes, but the feeling was incredible. Everything in the world felt right. Like I was somebody important. Not Rafter Bailey the regular kid. Rafter Bailey the unstoppable.

Benny leaned back, his eyes wide. He kept looking around the room like he'd just woken up in a ball pit filled with candy. I could see the wheels spinning in his head.

"So what have you been working on with Uncle John?" I asked. "Have you been giving him powers?"

Thimon shook his head. "He's got a broken leg. It wouldn't do much good to give him a power."

That made sense.

Thimon's voice took on a hard edge. "The Joneses are up to something. They spent years working in the dark. They came out, they attacked us, and then they went straight back into the dark again. They captured almost all of the superheroes, and now they want to finish the job. They probably think it's going to be easy."

"It is going to be easy," Benny said. "There are less than a hundred superheroes left. And we all have worthless powers."

"Right," Thimon said. "But now we have two surprises for them. Two things they aren't expecting."

"What's that?" Benny's voice was thick with awe.

"My powers," Thimon said, "and the two of you. Out of all the superheroes *in the country*, Split Rock was the only place that avoided the Joneses' attack. And the only reason Split Rock survived was because of you two."

"And Juanita," I said.

Thimon nodded. "And Juanita. But we can't tell her

about any of this. At least not yet."

I felt a pang of guilt. Juanita was my friend. She was part of the team. But I'd also just made a promise to Thimon.

I pushed that thought out of my head. Maybe I could convince Thimon to reconsider down the road.

Now, Thimon sounded determined. "Uncle John and I are working on finding the Joneses. The plan was to find them, and then use my powers to fight them. But maybe we can use my powers now, with you two, to help track them down. We could help find out what the Joneses are up to. Once we've done that, we could stop them. We could beat them."

Thimon seemed so sure of what he was saying. He looked strong and confident, with his arms folded across his chest. It might have helped that he was older. Right then, I would have followed Thimon into a minefield. This wasn't hunkering down. This wasn't hiding.

This was big. This was important.

This was exactly what superheroes did.

"I'll help out," I said. "However I can."

Benny hopped up to his feet. "That is so . . . awesome! Give us the powers. Right now, and we'll go get the Joneses. We'll have all of them by dinner."

"We don't even know where the Joneses are," I pointed out. "Besides, what would you do if you found them? We know there are a lot of Joneses, you can't conk them all on the heads."

"You're the one who always comes up with a good plan," Benny said. "We'll explode that bridge when we come to it." Benny turned to Thimon. "Can you give me the power to sing bass? I've always wanted to sing bass."

Thimon burst out laughing. "Um, no. That's not one of my seven powers, Benny. Sorry. But Rafter is right. It's dangerous to give you powers right now. We don't know how closely the Joneses are watching us. Before we strike, we have to find out as much as we can."

Suddenly, everything came into focus. For months there had been nothing to do, but now I had a mission. Something I could work on. My job was clear. It was like having a superhero checklist.

- Find the Joneses.
- Get a superpower.
- Beat the villains.

"Juanita," I blurted out. "I know we can't tell her about the powers, but she can help us find the Joneses. She's so brilliant, she can find anything on the internet."

Thimon looked doubtful.

"We can't leave her out of it," I said. "She's our friend."

Thimon didn't say anything for a long time. Benny had begun pacing the room, but now he stopped, and we both fell silent as we waited for a reply.

Thimon finally held out a fist. "Okay, let's do this. The four of us. We're going to track the Joneses down, we're going to confront them, and we're going to beat them. Agreed?"

I was grinning like an idiot. I put my own fist next to his, and Benny added his, too.

Thimon smiled. "The Baileys are going on the hunt."

4

IF I THROW UP, IT'S GOING TO BE A PUDDING RAINBOW

"The cafeteria workers are making a mockery of pizza day." Juanita poked at the lump of dough, red paste, and white globs on her plate. She held up a red, squishy mass with her fork. "Benny, what does this look like to you, a pepperoni or a stepped-on tomato?"

"Unfortunately, I'm not a pepperoni expert," Benny said. "But if you need to know anything about goat's milk, I'm your man."

Juanita dropped her fork and pushed her tray away. "I can't believe I'm about to say this, but today, your food looks better than mine."

Benny held out a baggie filled with jicama slices. "Do

you want some? I've got plenty."

Juanita shook her head and laughed. "No. I said it looks *better*, not good enough to eat."

Juanita glanced over my shoulder, smiled at someone, and waved. I turned around and saw Amit, a new kid at school, standing with his tray and looking for a place to sit.

I motioned for him to come sit with us. He smiled, waved nervously, and then went and sat by himself.

"Amit doesn't have any friends yet," Juanita said. "I've been trying to be nice, but I don't have any classes with him."

I frowned. Our table had space for ten students, but there were only the three of us. "I don't get it," I said. "Do people think we're geeks? Is this the geek table?"

Benny answered with his mouth full. "People may think this is the geek table, but you and I know full well what table it really is."

The superhero table.

I shrugged. I guess if people wanted to think we were geeks, there wasn't anything I could do about it. If they knew who we really were, they'd be swarming all over us, asking for autographs, maybe wanting us to take them flying or something.

Even though the Joneses knew who we were, secret identities were still good and necessary.

I finished my mashed potatoes and chard, put away my plastic container, and cleared my throat. "Juanita, Benny and I have something we want to discuss with you."

Benny nodded with enthusiasm, licking his spoon.

"I can't tell you everything, but there is something in the works. Something big."

Juanita's eyebrows lifted. "Really? What's going on?"

I leaned forward and Juanita did the same. "Benny and I are headed to the library after school. We've got to find out anything we can about the Joneses. Last time you were able—" I stopped. "Is something wrong?"

Juanita's face had fallen.

"Don't you remember what day it is?"

"Is it your birthday?" Benny said. "I can sing to you, but not in bass."

"No, it's not my birthday." Juanita sounded hurt. "It's Wednesday—the senior citizen center? Monroe is coming and I need your help."

I liked volunteering with Juanita. She had once said if you can't do something big and important, then you can at least do *something*. I liked that, but now with Thimon's powers, we *could* do something big and important. Suddenly volunteering seemed like something citizens should do. Not superheroes.

"Oh . . . yeah," I said. "That's right. Benny and I were planning on it, but . . ."

I had to think fast.

"Look, Juanita," Benny said. "What Rafter and I are working on . . . no offense, but it's way cooler than hanging out with the old people."

I jumped in before Benny could say anything else.

"We totally forgot that today was the day we're going to the senior center," I said. "But Benny and I are excited to go."

"We are?" Benny asked.

"What if we go there right after school?" I asked. "We can grab something to eat, and then spend some time at the library. Would that work?"

Juanita still didn't look thrilled, but she agreed. "We won't need to get something to eat. They always have pudding and snacks at the Terrace."

I nodded to Benny. Once we found where the Joneses were hiding, we could convince Juanita to go back to superhero work. To the big stuff.

I added another item to my superhero checklist:

- Hang out at a senior citizen center.

※

"I'm going to throw up. I'm not even kidding. I'm going to throw up all over the table."

I gave Benny a stern look. "I told you not to eat so much pudding. How many did you have, six?"

"At least a dozen." Benny moaned. "I had chocolate,

vanilla, and banana. If I throw up, it's going to be a pudding rainbow."

Benny leaned forward and rested his head on the table. He let out another groan. "When I burp, it smells like medicine and crossword puzzles."

"That's what you get for breaking the superhero diet," I said.

"There was a small possibility the pudding was made out of goat's milk," Benny replied. "Speaking of that, I need to get home so I can feed my goats."

"You know those goats are just pretend, right, Benny?" I asked.

"Yes," Benny said. "But they have feelings. Virtual feelings. When I'm gone, they miss me."

I pulled out my phone and checked the time. We'd been at the senior center all of twenty minutes. We still had forty minutes left to go.

I checked the bite marks on my ankle. Monroe had bitten me before Juanita roped him into a chess tournament. He was currently trash-talking a World War II veteran in the corner, even though the old man was beating him soundly.

Juanita left a group of people who were putting together a puzzle and came over.

"Hey, guys." She smiled. "It's even more fun when you actually . . . you know . . . talk to the people."

Benny groaned and burped.

I looked around the room. There were several groups playing games at a few tables. Others were cross-stitching and talking. A group of men and women were tying a quilt. I almost wished Monroe would start biting my ankle again, just to liven things up.

"Sorry, Juanita," I said. "Benny and I are used to more . . . action than this."

Juanita pointed to three women set apart from the others. "If you want action, you should go join those ladies in the corner."

One of the women was playing a game of solitaire. Another knitted, and a third had a roll of yarn she was winding into a ball. They were speaking quietly, but looked pretty animated.

"Whoa," I said, holding up my hands in mock protest. "Let's not get crazy. I don't think even Benny and I could handle that much excitement. I mean, look at that. One of them is making a yarn ball! Yeehaw!"

Juanita gave me a stern look. "The woman playing cards is a Bailey. The two with yarn are Johnsons." Juanita glanced around, then leaned forward and lowered her voice. "If you really want to learn about the family business, you should go and talk to three ladies who have lived their entire lives as superheroes."

"What do you think?" I asked Benny.

My brother let out a rather loud belch. He pounded

himself on the chest. "There we go. The pudding is tucked safely into bed. Sure. Let's go talk to them."

Benny and I wandered over to the ladies. When it was clear we were walking toward them, they stopped all conversation and focused on their yarn and cards.

"Uh . . . ," I said. "My name is Rafter, and this is my brother Benny. We're here to . . ." To be honest, I had no idea why we were there. "We're here to talk."

The woman with the yarn ball didn't even look up from her project. "That's nice, boys. But we're doing just fine on our own."

There was a second of awkward silence.

"We're Baileys," Benny said.

They suddenly became much nicer.

"Oh, that's wonderful!"

"Come sit down, you can help me with my solitaire."

"We thought we were going to have to stop our reminiscing, but you'll fit right in."

Benny joined the woman playing cards. I sat next to the lady with the yarn ball, whose name was Merry.

Merry motioned to the other two women. "Barbara and Judith were just discussing the communist uprising in South America. We seem to be a little fuzzy on the exact dates and details."

"I'm telling you," Judith said, her knitting needles never slowing down. Her gray hair was curled and piled on top of her head like a beehive. "It was nineteen-hundred and forty-six. I remember because of the locusts."

"The locusts?" Barbara said. "Was nineteen-hundred and forty-six the only year they had locusts?"

"No, but Bolivia was especially damp in forty-six. Cochabamba alone had over two inches in April. You know what they say—water in April, locusts in May."

"Two inches sounds to me like average rainfall for Cochabamba," Barbara said. She laid a card on the table and drew another from the top of the deck. "Tell her, Merry. And it wasn't Bolivia where they had the uprising, it was Cameroon."

"Ha!" Judith burst. "Cameroon is in Africa. It's a little hard to have a South American communist uprising in the heart of Africa. Tell her, Merry."

The two continued arguing, and Merry leaned over to me. "I tend to stay out of these discussions. My memory isn't what it used to be, and I'm not so good at making up statistics."

I wasn't so good at talking with adults. But there was something about Merry that put me at ease. Her hair was cut short and she wore horn-rimmed glasses that were connected to a beaded necklace. Her fingers worked deftly as she rolled the yarn into a larger and larger ball.

I tried to think of something interesting to talk about. "Where are you from?"

"Do you mean now, or before all of this craziness happened?" Merry asked, and then went right on talking without waiting for an answer. "I used to live in Phoenix. Judith, Barbara, and I shared the same nursing home. Then one day we got worthless powers and suddenly nobody was visiting us anymore. We called around and found out you nice folks in Split Rock had escaped the attack, so we moved down here. Still in a nursing home, of course." She motioned to Juanita. "She's quite the girl, you know. Taking time out of her busy day to come and visit us old and worthless superheroes."

"You're not old and worthless," I protested. But to be honest, it sounded uncomfortably close to how Benny and I had been describing them just a few moments before.

"You can't argue with facts," she said, smiling. "All three of us are old. And our worthless powers are especially worthless. When Barbara snaps, it sounds like bagpipes. Judith can sneeze and keep her eyes open at the same time. All I can do is grow a mustache on my left kneecap."

I saw Benny's eyes go wide, and he opened his mouth, probably to ask if he could see the mustache. I shook my head at him. He scowled and went back to playing cards.

"No, sir," Merry said. "Our days of being useful are long gone."

"It's not your power that makes you super," I said. "It's what you do with that power."

Merry stopped her rolling. She looked at me over her glasses. "That's quite a profound thought from somebody still wet behind the ears."

My face felt warm. "It's something my grandpa said."

"Well, your grandpa sounds like a smart man."

Benny asked Judith what she was knitting.

"I'm knitting anti-chafing pads," she said. "Have you ever worn supersuits?"

Benny scowled and shook his head.

"The chafing is horrible, especially during the wet months." She held up one of her pads. It was about the size of a pancake. "Pin one of these to your tights, and your chafing worries are over."

"Superheroes don't chafe," Benny said.

Judith looked like she was about to argue, but just then Juanita came up behind us. "Sorry to break things up, ladies. Your bus is here to take you back to Sunshine Terrace."

"Ah, man," Benny complained. "It was just getting interesting."

Benny brought over Merry's walker, and we helped the women out to the bus. We said good-bye and promised to see them again, and Monroe even gave Merry a hug. Then, as soon as the bus drove away, Monroe kicked me once in the shins and ran off, whooping and hollering.

"Well," Juanita said. "Do you guys want to come in and help clean up?"

"Can't the other people take care of that?" Benny asked. "We need to get working on the important stuff."

Juanita had turned to go back inside, but Benny's comment made her freeze.

"That's not what he meant," I jumped in, trying to save Benny. "It's just . . ." I couldn't tell Juanita about Thimon's powers. I'd promised. "Benny and I are tired of hunkering down. It's time we find out where the Joneses are hiding so we can do something important."

Juanita faced Benny and me. The frosty look on her face made me take a step back.

"You both keep using that word," Juanita said. "*Important*. Are you saying what I'm doing isn't important?"

"No," I protested. "This is all really good. It's just . . . not very big. I mean, you're helping a few people at a nursing home. But what we're working on . . . it could save the whole city."

It had been fun to talk to Merry and the other ladies, but this seemed so obvious to me. Hanging out at the senior center was small and unimportant. I was a superhero. I wanted to do something bigger.

Juanita took a step toward me, her face angry. "There

are over eighty superheroes in this city. They've been here for three months. And do you know what we've done in that time?"

I shook my head.

"Nothing."

"Exactly!" I said. "That's what Benny and I are trying to change."

"Three months," Juanita continued. "We don't even go on patrol any more. Did you know that crime is on the rise?"

Juanita looked from me to Benny and then back to me. "You said we should leave the little stuff to the citizens— that we should focus on the big stuff. But we haven't even done little stuff! We spent years fighting each other, damaging the city, and once we find a real threat, we go into hiding! We act like we're powerless."

That made me angry. "Juanita, if you hadn't noticed, we *are* powerless."

Even as my mouth said it, my brain told me it was a mistake. Juanita looked like I'd slapped her in the face.

I braced myself. Juanita was already angry, and now I was ready for her fury.

But that isn't what happened. Juanita's shoulders dropped and she looked down at the ground.

I felt like a bully right then. "Juanita . . . ," I said. "I'm sorry, I didn't mean—"

My friend turned her back on me and walked off.

I thought about going after her, but I didn't know what else to say. What I'd said was true.

"What do you think, Benny?" I looked over at my brother.

"I think I want more pudding."

I sighed, rubbing my forehead with my hand. "We might have to go on this adventure without Juanita."

✳

On the way home, Benny and I saw an old man get his briefcase stolen by a man wearing a hoodie. Nobody stopped the man as he raced down the subway stairs. I stopped at a newspaper stand and read the front-page headline:

CRIME SOARS

We spent the night looking for information about the Joneses on the internet. We found nothing.

The next day was the last day of school. Usually that was a big event, but I hardly even noticed what we did. There were more important things going on. To make matters worse, Juanita didn't show up.

When we got home, we spent more time on the internet with the same results. The Joneses were nowhere to be found.

It was hopeless without Juanita.

That night at dinner, Dad got a call from Grandpa. Dad hung up and told us the news.

"Uncle Ralph, Aunt Carole, and Cousin Jessie have gone missing."

TODAY YOU MUST EXCEL AT HUNKERING DOWN

Now we knew. The Joneses were on the move.

But so were the Baileys. Of course, the Joneses were probably more organized.

"Benny, stop bumping me."

"You're doing it wrong. Here, let me."

"Boys, both of you back up."

Dad pulled us away from the piano in the living room. He played the first few lines of Beethoven's Bagatelle in A Minor, and a secret door opened in the living room. After a little more pushing, which ended with us just letting Benny lead the way, Rodney, Benny, Dad, and I all filed downstairs into the root cellar. Mom and Thimon stayed upstairs to clear the dishes.

Our root cellar wasn't an ordinary root cellar. Actually, to be honest, I didn't even know what a real root cellar looked like. But our root cellar was a large underground area where we kept our secret super equipment.

We all filed into Rodney's computer room.

"How is the technology stuff coming?" Dad asked. "Have you gotten anything back online?"

Rodney sat down at his keyboard. There were empty energy-drink cans and snack-cake wrappers cluttered around the desk and floor. He wiggled the mouse and began to type.

"It's complicated." Rodney pointed to a large computer hard drive under the table. "As soon as I get this computer online, we'll be able to share all our strategic systems again, but we'll also be vulnerable to the Joneses. If they hack us, they'd have access to everything—bank accounts, identities, the location of our headquarters. I have to be sure that we're secure before I put us back online."

"All right," Dad said. "You're the computer expert. You know what's best."

Rodney's new power didn't exactly help him get things working again. He had the ability to stop his fingernails from growing.

Rodney pulled out a rectangular touchpad the size of a phone. "For now, the only way for anybody to access the stuff on this computer is if they are in this room, and if they are me."

He put two fingers on the pad. A voice sounded over the speakers. *Handprint recognized. Please enter your password.*

Rodney typed in a password long enough to be a paragraph. In another moment he had the Bailey family locator app pulled up on the screen. The locator showed where every superhero in the city was.

"According to this, Uncle Ralph, Aunt Carole, and Cousin Jesse are at the movies," Rodney said. "Riverside Plaza. Except . . ."

"Except what?" I said.

"Except this says they've been there for nine hours."

"Nine hours?" Benny asked. "Maybe they're sneaking into different theaters to watch a bunch of movies."

"That's definitely against the superhero code," Dad said. "Riverside Plaza is close to us. I'll head out there and call Grandpa on the way. You boys sit tight. Don't leave the house and don't answer the door. Today you must excel at hunkering down. I'll call you as soon as I find out anything."

"I don't want to hunker." Benny chased after Dad. "Can't I come with you?"

"Sorry, son!" Dad called over his shoulder. "You don't have your supersuit yet."

Benny returned to the room grumbling. "Stupid super-suits."

We waited. Rodney messed around on his computer. I watched, even though I didn't understand any of it. Benny twirled his chair around in circles and then tried to walk across the room with his eyes closed. He finally stopped after he ran into the wall with his head.

"Hey, guys." Rodney sat up suddenly, his eyes bright. "Do you want to see the latest progress on the device?"

He didn't have to explain which device. Rodney had been trying to rebuild the device October Jones had used to take away our powers. We'd recovered it from the dump after our battle, and Rodney had been painstakingly trying to figure out how it worked.

We followed him into the next room. I'd seen the device in various stages—a jumbled chunk of metal; laid out in pieces; partially rebuilt—but now, it looked like Rodney had created an all-new device that only barely resembled the old one.

"Does it work?" Benny reached out to touch it, but Rodney swatted his hand away.

"Um, don't you think if I had it working I would have mentioned it?" Rodney said. Still, I could tell he was proud of the work he'd done.

"It looks like it should work," I said. "What's missing?"

Rodney sighed. "All the pieces are back together, but I

wasn't able to save any of the code from the drive. Without that, it's like a car without an engine. It looks nice, but it doesn't do anything."

"Any chance of writing the code yourself?"

Rodney shook his head. "I don't think I could do that even with my superpower. The only way to get the code is to hack into the Joneses' computer systems. Of course, before we can do that, we have to know where their systems actually are. We don't even know where the Joneses themselves are, let alone their computers."

Rodney made it sound like we were light-years away from defeating the Joneses. But to me, it felt like we were so close. I could see the checklist in my head.

"We have to hit the library tomorrow," I told Benny.

"But school is out," Benny said. "It's summer. I've got to start sleeping in."

"If we don't find the Joneses, the Joneses will find us. I don't want that to happen."

Rodney's phone rang. He answered it, listened, asked a few questions, and then hung up.

"Dad found their cell phones in the trash can in a Dumpster behind the theater. It seems pretty obvious. The Joneses got them."

6

I'M THINKING I NEED TO TAKE UP TAXIDERMY

"It's hopeless."

A few days passed with no new developments. I finally got tired of sitting around at home, so we got special permission to go to the library. Mom and Dad weren't happy about it, but we'd promised not to go anywhere else. We spent two hours looking at old newspapers that weren't online. Twice I caught Benny playing the goat game on his phone. Needless to say, we hadn't found anything.

I'd texted Juanita four times. Once to apologize, twice to invite her to the library, and once to ask her if she'd been kidnapped by the Joneses. I'd added a smiley face to the last text.

She hadn't replied to any of them.

"Come on," I told Benny. "It's time to go home."

Benny opened his backpack and passed over a hat and sunglasses to me, then put on his own hat and sunglasses. The only way Mom and Dad let us go out is if we wore this disguise. The hat and sunglasses were meant to keep us hidden. I think it made us stand out more than anything.

We walked out onto the street and headed toward the bus stop. All the while, I chewed over the information we'd found. Or rather, hadn't found. Jones was such a common name. There was all kinds of information about Joneses, but how could you tell who was a regular citizen and who was a supervillain?

I was so caught up in my thoughts, I didn't even notice when Benny disappeared. One minute he was walking next to me, the next, he was gone. My heart froze and I spun around, ready to chase, tackle, or fight.

Benny was standing on the sidewalk, his face toward the sky.

"Benny," I said, a little angry that he'd scared me. "What're you doing?"

My brother pointed at the skyscraper he was looking up at. "It's the Baylor," he said. "The tallest hotel in the city. Sometimes I like to look at all the windows and imagine the people behind them. People visiting from out of town. On business trips. Maybe some of them are looking down at us, and we look like ants."

Benny waved up at the hotel.

I sighed. "That's great, but we really need to get home."

A scream from behind made me spin on my heels. It took only a split second to see what was happening.

Across the street, a man wearing a ski mask raced down the sidewalk. An older woman chased after him, waving her hands and yelling.

"My purse! He stole my purse!" The woman wore heels and would never be able to catch him.

There wasn't a police officer in sight. A few people stood shocked on the sidewalk, but nobody made a move to stop the mugger. I saw why. He was carrying a knife. It looked like he'd used it to cut the strap on the purse, and now he was waving the weapon in front of him.

I didn't have a supersuit. I didn't have a power. But I couldn't just stand there. Benny stepped up to stand by my side.

"That guy looks like he needs a good conk."

I nodded. We couldn't stop him as superheroes, but we could stop him as regular citizens. We sprang off the sidewalk and into the street.

Something caught my attention out of the corner of my eye—an older boy standing by a van that said ROYLANCE'S TACOS on the side. The boy had angled himself so the mugger couldn't see him.

The boy looked familiar, and he motioned me back with one hand. I grabbed Benny by the arm.

"Look." I pointed at the Roylance's Tacos van. "Who's that?"

"I don't know," Benny said. "But the bad guy's getting away."

The mugger almost ran right past the van, but the boy stepped out at the last second and tripped him. A second figure leaped out of the van—a girl, about the same age as the boy. She kicked the knife out of the mugger's hand, and it went flying. The boy jumped on top of the man and pinned his arms to his sides, and just like that, the fight was over.

The two of them had stopped a mugging.

The girl pulled out her cell phone to call the police. The boy held the mugger against the pavement, and he looked over at Benny and me. I could see the smile from across the street. He nodded like we were old friends at school, and then . . . then he turned his head, spat, and grinned.

I grinned, too. I raised my hand in a fist and shook it.

"It looks like a few other people are tired of hunkering down," I said. "We're all finding ways to fight back. I bet Roylance's Taco van is some kind of mobile undercover vehicle the Johnsons have."

Benny nodded. "I got to get me one of those."

✳

Back home, I wadded up a piece of scratch paper and threw it at the garbage. Something about the act of balling up the paper made me feel good. Like I was crushing the Joneses' plans. I tried not to think about the truth—that the only thing I'd been able to do on my superhero checklist was visit a retirement home.

I threw another wad of paper with enough force to bounce against the wall and land on Benny's bed.

"Hey," Benny said, kicking the paper to the floor. He looked back to his phone.

"Haven't you gotten bored of that goat game yet?" I asked.

"Yes." Benny sounded guilty. "It's actually very boring, but I can't stop. My farm has almost five hundred goats and three hundred acres. If I stop feeding and watering the goats, they'll all die."

I balled up another paper and was about to throw it at Benny when my phone buzzed.

I glanced at the screen. A message from Juanita.

Check your email. I'm sorry.

I went to my desk and pulled up my email.

Rafter,

I'm sorry. You're right. You have been helping me out the past few months, and it was selfish of me not to help you. I am your friend, and friends are there for each

other. No matter what. I've attached everything I can find on the Joneses. It's not much, but maybe it's a place to get started.

I heard about your other relatives. We had a family go missing this morning too. Six Johnsons, all gone. Grandmother called everybody in to headquarters and won't let me leave. I'll contact you again as soon as I can.
Your friend,
Juanita

The note made me sad, and it took me a moment to realize why.

Friends are there for each other. No matter what.

I didn't understand why Juanita wanted to help out at the food pantry and the senior center. But she did. If I was a real friend, I would have been there for her. Instead, I'd told her she wasn't doing things that were important.

And now she'd apologized to me.

The next time I saw her, I would make this right. I promised myself.

Opening the attachment, I saw a seventeen-page document. It had articles, pictures, and links to a few websites. None of this information had come up in my searches.

I hit the print button and then had to go all the way down to the root cellar to get the pages. I took them up to

Thimon's room and knocked on his door.

"Come in," Thimon called from inside.

I entered the room. Thimon had his laptop open on his desk.

"How is it going?" I asked. "Have you found anything?"

Thimon shook his head. "Nope. I've hit a dead end. I have no idea where to go from here. What about you guys? Any luck?"

"Benny and I struck out at the library," I said. "However, Juanita may have found something. I haven't had a chance to look at it closely yet."

I handed the papers to Thimon, who cleared a place on his desk and spread them out. He glanced through them, frowned, and then started reading them again.

I sat on the bed. Thimon continued to read, rubbing his forehead every once in a while. After a few minutes, he started mumbling to himself.

"How did she . . . I didn't even think . . . that clever girl."

Thimon finally looked up. "Well, this is more than I thought was possible. I mean, it's not a road map to where the Joneses are hiding, but it's a definite start. She's found a shell company that looks like it may lead to the Jones family right here in Split Rock. I didn't even know this kind of information was public."

"Shell company?" I asked.

Thimon nodded. "Yeah. A fake company that is set up to hide illegal activity. Somehow she managed to dig it up." Thimon stood up and walked to the window, looking out. After a moment, he turned around.

"Can you give me a minute? I'm going to call Uncle John and see what he thinks about all of this."

"Oh, sure." I went back to my room.

Benny was playing on his phone. "I'm thinking I need to take up taxidermy," Benny said. "That's a skill that will take you far in life."

"Taxidermy?" I asked. "You mean like with bears and deer and stuff?"

"Well, I wouldn't want to hurt animals," Benny said. "I was thinking more like a vegetarian taxidermist. You know. Celery, jicama. Things like that."

Thimon came in and closed the door behind him. He looked excited.

"Uncle John thinks your friend has discovered something," Thimon said. My heart skipped a beat. "Who found this again?"

"Juanita," I said. "She's the one who helped us last spring. When we fought October Jones."

Thimon nodded. "Ah, so that's Juanita. Okay. That's good. I think we have enough to go on. Are you guys ready for your first assignment?"

"I can't." Benny held up his phone. "If I don't get the north fields planted with okra, my goats are going to starve come winter."

A sly smile crept across Thimon's mouth. "What if the assignment involves giving the two of you superpowers?"

Benny jumped up and tossed his phone on the bed. It was the last anybody heard of his virtual goats.

7

I'D LOVE A GOOD FIGHT WITH A NINJA

I had high hopes. I figured Thimon would give us the superpowers, and we'd be conking Joneses on the head by suppertime. But that's not how it happened.

Thimon locked the bedroom door. He sat down and motioned for us to sit next to him. I could tell the last thing Benny wanted to do was sit down, but he followed Thimon's directions.

Thimon reached out and touched us both on the forehead. I felt a slight shock. I wasn't sure if it was static electricity, or if it had to do with Thimon's power.

"I don't feel any different," Benny said.

"I haven't given you a power yet," Thimon said. "But I

had to make a mental connection to both of you."

Benny was rocking back and forth in anticipation. "Okay, so what now? What's next?"

"Well, now you ask me for a power," Thimon said. "I have seven of them—flame, lightning, speed, strength, frost, supersight, and flying."

"Speed," Benny said immediately. "Give me speed."

"Rafter?" Thimon looked at me.

I almost said strength, but I couldn't exactly start destroying things in my bedroom.

I looked out the window. "Flight," I replied.

"Flight and speed," Thimon said. "Coming right up."

Thimon snapped his fingers, and I felt a warm tingling in my feet. The feeling spread up my legs and into the rest of my body. It was the same feeling I'd had when I first got my worthless power. And then again when I'd gotten my real power.

Something clicked in my mind. The new power washed over me, and in an instant I knew how to use it. I knew everything about flying.

I rose off the floor—still sitting cross-legged—grinning like a fool.

I felt *power*. Not just the power of flight, but the power that comes from being super. I could do something that nobody else could do. I was no longer Rafter-without-his-power. I was Rafter Hans Bailey . . . superhero.

I floated up until my head touched the ceiling, plans racing through my mind the entire time.

Benny stood up and looked around the room, his face panicked. "I can't run in here or I'll knock something over. I'm going outside."

"Wait," Thimon said. "There are a few rules."

"Aw, man," Benny complained. "Every time something good happens, there have to be rules."

"Before we take on the Joneses, you have to learn how to use your powers," Thimon said. "We're going to practice for a few days, but remember, it's important to stay hidden. We can't lose the element of surprise."

He stood and went over to his backpack. He unzipped one of the pockets and retrieved a small plastic case, which he held out to us. "Take one of these."

The case held three black objects, each shaped like teeth and about the same size.

I lowered myself to the floor and took one of the objects. It was soft and foamy, with a solid center. "What are these?"

Thimon put one of the objects in his ear. "It's a micro-earpiece. This'll let us talk to each other. It has a range of about twenty miles, so don't wander too far."

Benny grabbed the last earpiece and shoved it in his ear.

"Wait, you're not coming with us?"

Thimon shook his head. "I have to stay here, where it's safe. If something were to happen to me while you were flying a thousand feet in the sky . . . that could be bad."

Benny went over to the window and yanked it open. "Rafter," he called over his shoulder. "There's no time for stairs. Fly me out to somewhere I can run."

Benny's enthusiasm was contagious, but I remembered what Thimon had just said. "Benny, we can't fly out the window, we'd give away our superpowers."

To my surprise, Thimon said it was fine. "Just fly straight up and fly fast. Nobody will see you. Once you're high enough, we'll find somewhere secluded."

"How about the canyon?" Benny asked. "There's lots of places up there that you can't get to by car. We'd be all alone."

I nodded. "Benny's right. Lots of trees. Nobody would see us. We could practice our powers there."

"Okay," Thimon said. "You both have your earpieces. You're good to go."

Benny climbed out onto the roof and I followed. I made sure none of the neighbors were in their backyards. We were alone.

I grabbed Benny under the arms. "Ready?" I asked.

Benny grinned and gave me a thumbs-up.

I looked once more around the neighborhood, and

then leaped into the sky.

I cannot find the right words to describe the feeling. I'd flown before—many times with Dad. But this was different. I was in control. There was nothing between me and the ground. My feet dangled. The sky surrounded me in a brilliant blue. Benny whooped like a little kid who'd just gotten a pony for his birthday.

I flew straight up at first, high enough so that no one could see us from the ground. Then I soared. I banked first to the left, and then to the right. I let out a yell that drowned out even Benny's hollering.

This is what it meant to be super. Doing something nobody else could do.

I could hear Thimon laughing through the earpiece. "Glad you guys are having fun, but maybe it's time to head up to the canyon. I have a feeling you'll need to know each power before we can fight the Joneses."

I got my bearings and flew toward the mountain range, dropping lower as we got close. I flew past the dam at the base of the canyon, and then farther into the mountains. I found a secluded meadow and dropped Benny down on the ground. Before I could say a word, he'd disappeared. All that was left was a trail of dust that showed which way he'd run.

"Benny!" I laughed, assuming he could hear me through

the earpiece. "Come back. Let's practice together."

With a rush of air and a skid of pebbles, Benny came racing back.

"You know what this canyon needs?" Benny grinned.

"What's that?" I asked.

"Ninjas," Benny said. "I'd love a good fight with a ninja."

"Yeah, I heard this place is overflowing with the dreaded tree ninja," I said, smiling.

✳

We practiced. I wanted to be fighting Joneses, but Thimon was right. First we had to practice.

There was a lot to learn with each power. For example, when you had strength, you couldn't just lift boulders into the air. You had to have the right balance and grip. Most boulders didn't come with handles.

With speed you had to be aware what kind of surface you were on so you knew how long it would take to slow down or speed up. With fire you could make large orange explosions that burned out quickly, or small, focused, white fire that cut like a welder's flame.

Perhaps most important, Benny and I learned how to work together. Having one person with a superpower was good. Having two people with superpowers was even better. But the best was when we combined our two powers to do things that surprised even Thimon.

One move involved me having strength and Benny

having lightning. I would whirl Benny around like I was a discus thrower and then hurl him into the air. He could fire bolts of lightning from a high vantage point, and then at the last second, ask Thimon for flight. He'd return to me and we'd start all over again. It was like having a superhero who had flight and lightning at the same time.

By dinnertime we were exhausted. Exhausted, but thrilled. For the first time since my encounter with October, I felt super again. We hadn't fought a battle. We hadn't come any closer to finding the Joneses. But we had powers, and we were learning how to use them. That was the first step.

It was exhilarating, and I wanted to do it again. And again. I could have spent forever in that canyon.

Thimon's voice came over the earpiece. It sounded like he was shouting to somebody else. "We'll be right out!" His voice returned to normal. "Your parents are calling us for dinner. You guys better come home fast."

The power of flight rushed through me. I picked up Benny and leaped into the air. It took only a few minutes before Benny and I were crawling through the window again.

Thimon touched our foreheads again to break his mental connection.

"That was totally wild," Benny said. "We have *got* to go out again after dinner."

Thimon grinned. "We'll see. You guys picked up on things very quickly."

Mom was setting dinner on the table. Dad was finishing up the cooking. "Did you boys have fun playing up in your room?" Mom asked.

My stomach dropped. Thimon looked at me and gave a small shake of his head. I didn't like the idea of keeping information from Mom. But I'd made a promise to Thimon.

"Yeah, Mom." I said. "It's been a pretty uneventful Sunday afternoon."

I ate my mashed potatoes and chard, but they tasted . . . off.

I knew why. A few hours ago I'd felt invincible. I had superpowers again. We were practicing to beat the Joneses. And then . . .

It's been a pretty uneventful Sunday afternoon.

I think the day would have been perfect, if it hadn't been for the little lie I'd had to tell.

8

I'D CHOOSE THE BEAR

We spent the next three days practicing out in the canyon. Mom commented that we were spending a lot of time "in our room," but it was easy enough to change the subject whenever she asked us about it.

Even though Benny and I were getting better and better, Thimon seemed to be more and more nervous. He spent a lot of time talking to Uncle John on the phone. Finally, on Tuesday night, he came into our room, carrying the papers I'd printed out from Juanita. I'd almost forgotten about them.

"Do you know if Juanita is still looking for the Joneses?" Thimon asked. "And do you know if she's shared this information with anybody else?"

I shook my head. "I'm not sure about either one. I haven't spoken to her since she gave that to us."

I felt a stab of guilt. I hadn't called or texted Juanita. I'd all but forgotten her. Benny and I had been busy with our new powers.

Thimon rubbed his chin. It looked like he hadn't shaved in a few days. "Well, I can't send all this stuff to Uncle John over regular email because the Joneses might intercept it. Your brother still hasn't got the secure email up and running, right?"

I shook my head. Juanita had sent it over regular email, but Thimon was right. We didn't want to take any more risks than we had to.

"You'll have to meet Juanita somewhere," Thimon said.

I continued to shake my head. "Can't do that. Her whole family is on lockdown. And besides, I don't think I could convince her anyway."

"Why do we need her?" Benny asked. "I thought you could only give powers to two people at once. I don't want to have to take turns."

"We can't tell her about the powers," Thimon said. "We just need to talk to her . . . to see if she can find anything else about the Joneses."

I frowned. "Well, we can give it a shot," I said. "But I can't make any promises."

*

Over the next two days, I talked with Juanita over email. Apparently, part of being on lockdown meant her grandmother had taken her phone. Because we were talking through regular email, though, we had to talk in . . . general terms. I would ask Juanita if she could meet to "talk about summer reading." And Juanita would tell me that her grandmother wouldn't let her come out and play.

Thimon kept pushing, until finally he said there was no point in practicing with the powers if we couldn't get Juanita's help. Upon hearing that we might not get to practice, Benny begged me to do whatever I had to in order for Juanita to agree to meet.

I hated to do it, but I wrote Juanita a very short message.

Hi, Juanita.
I know your grandmother doesn't want you to come out and play, but this is very important. I'm asking you as a friend. Can you meet us downtown? At Edlund Park?
Rafter

I knew she'd understand what I was saying. *Friends are there for each other. No matter what.* That night I had a reply from her.

Rafter,
I'll be there. At noon. Meet me by the statue of the guy
fighting a bear. Look for the Roylance's Taco van.
Your friend,
Juanita

Thimon patted me on the back and told me good work.
Benny gave me a high five. But when they left, I stared at
my computer screen and read the email again.

I felt sick to my stomach. I'd used my friendship with
Juanita for my own selfish purposes. I was making her do
something she didn't want to do. Had she gotten permission
to leave her headquarters, or was she going to sneak out?

At least I'd get to see her, face to face. I could apologize
for what I'd said at the senior center, and explain everything
in person. If she didn't want to get involved, I wouldn't push
her, no matter what Thimon and Benny said.

✳

"Why do we have to take the bus?" Benny asked. "Why
can't we just . . . you know?"

I couldn't answer Benny because we were surrounded
by people, but Thimon could. His voice came through our
earpieces.

"You can't just fly into the middle of Edlund Park, Benny.
Everybody would see you. I can give you powers, but only
in an emergency."

"We'd be fine if we had our s—" Benny stopped short.

"Your supersuits," Thimon said. "I know. Actually, I'm working on that. We have a bunch back in Three Forks that aren't being used anymore. Uncle John is going to see if he can ship two up here that would fit you."

Benny's eyes went wide and his mouth fell open. I could tell he wanted to get up and dance. His knee started bouncing up and down.

I looked around the bus. There were twelve other people sitting and standing around. One man had headphones on, his eyes closed. A woman stared at a magazine. It took me a moment to realize that she wasn't reading it. At least, it didn't look like she was. Her eyes stared blankly at the pages, never wavering. She never turned a page.

I looked at the other passengers. All of them seemed . . . distant. Almost like their minds were on something else. Or maybe on nothing else.

"This is our stop." Benny slapped my arm. We got off and walked the three blocks to the park and found the statue of the man wrestling the bear. Juanita hadn't arrived.

I found a bench and sat down. Benny went over to the statue and examined the plaque.

The park was relatively empty. I could see a few people playing Frisbee in the distance. Some runners were jogging away from us. But we had this part of the park to ourselves.

Benny came and sat down beside me.

"What did the plaque say?" I asked.

"It says this guy named Herman Wallbanger wrestled a bear one time and stole a fish right out of its mouth."

"I guess you didn't have to do much back then to get a statue made of you."

Benny waved behind me. "Juanita! Over here."

I turned and saw Juanita coming toward me. She walked with a slight hunch, as if she were carrying an invisible backpack on her shoulders. Something seemed . . . off.

"Hey, Juanita," I said. "Is everything okay?"

Juanita nodded. Her eyes seemed to look right through me.

"I can't stay long," she said. "My parents don't know I've left. I have to get back."

I remembered the promise I'd made to myself. To make things right. "I'm sorry, Juanita. I didn't mean for you to—"

"I've found more information about the Joneses. A lot more. I've copied about a hundred files on this drive." She held out a flash drive. I took it and looked at it. It was black with a silver stripe around the outside. I slipped it into my pocket.

My job had been to convince Juanita to help us find more information about the Joneses, but she'd already done just what we needed. "Juanita, that's incredible. Thank you."

"I have to go now." Juanita turned.

Something wasn't right. "Juanita, wait."

She turned back and faced me. She still didn't seem to want to look me in the eye.

"What's going on? What's wrong?"

She shook her head. "Nothing is wrong." There was an awkward moment of silence.

"Look," I said. "If we can find where the Joneses are located, Benny and I—" I couldn't tell her about the powers. I'd made a promise. But Juanita was my friend. Maybe even my best friend. "We're going to try to stop them. Will you help us?"

Juanita considered this for a while before responding. "Okay. But right now, I really have to get back. Look on that flash drive as soon as you can. It's important."

She turned, and I watched her go.

"Is it just me, or was Juanita acting a little strange?" I asked.

Benny nodded. "She looked a little scary. I think if I had to choose between wrestling Juanita and wrestling a bear, I'd choose the bear. Well, unless Juanita had a fish in her mouth. Then it's a toss-up."

Thimon spoke in my ear. "Her whole family is on lockdown and she snuck out. She's probably just afraid and wants to get back."

"Juanita is a lot of things," Benny said. "But I've never seen her afraid. Not even that time Rafter told her to fight a giant Jones guy with a van."

My brother was right. Juanita was as fearless as Benny. She wouldn't be nervous just because she'd sneaked out of her headquarters. I touched the flash drive in my pocket. Whatever was on here must be truly terrifying.

✳

Benny and I caught the bus home. Thimon was waiting for us. He touched our foreheads and broke the connection.

"She gave you a flash drive?" Thimon asked.

I nodded, stood up, and touched my pocket. I felt a moment of panic. The flash drive wasn't there.

"Did you put it in your backpack?" Thimon asked.

"I don't think so." I couldn't believe Juanita had gone to all the trouble to give me a flash drive, and I'd lost it.

I opened my backpack and sighed with relief. I held up the drive. "I must have dropped it in here on the bus. Let's get this to Rodney and see what Juanita has found."

The three of us made our way down to the root cellar. I felt a small headache coming on, and wondered if it had anything to do with the mental connection from Thimon.

"How's it going, Rodney?" I asked when we got to the computer room. Benny and Thimon crowded in behind me.

"It's going terrible," he said. "I'm trying to install three updates to the antivirus software, but I can't do it because the current antivirus software thinks I'm trying to install a virus."

I saw the device October had used to give us dud powers. I knew it was pointless to ask, but I had to. "Any chance that thing is working yet?"

Rodney looked at the device, looked at me, and then turned back to his screen. I knew it was bad if he wasn't even going to answer my questions.

I pulled out the flash drive Juanita had given me and held it up. Rodney plucked it out of my hand.

"What's this?" he said. "Where'd you get it?"

"Juanita," I answered. "She said there's some important information about the Joneses on here. It may give us a clue as to where they are."

Rodney looked at me over his glasses. "It's not safe to go plopping random flash drives into the main computer. You're sure this is from Juanita?"

I took it back and looked at it. It was the same drive Juanita had given me.

I nodded.

"I've disconnected this computer from the internet for three months because we can't let anybody break into this computer," Rodney said.

"She handed it to me herself," I replied. "About an hour ago."

Rodney gave me one more look. "What were you guys

doing out of the house on your own?"

"It's okay, I was with them," Thimon said.

"All right then, let's see what we've got." He turned to his computer and slipped the flash drive into the USB slot.

At first, nothing happened. Rodney pressed a few keys, and then . . . more nothing happened.

"That's strange," Rodney scooted closer to the keyboard. He moved the mouse, then tapped a few more keys.

The screen went blank.

"Gah!" Rodney leaned over and yanked the flash drive from the computer, and then turned to the screen. The monitor came back on but remained black, and code started scrolling by faster than I could read.

Rodney gasped.

"What is it?" Thimon asked. "What's going on?"

"This is why computers should only be used to play video games," Benny said.

Rodney jammed keys on the keyboard, but nothing changed. The code kept scrolling. He reached down and unplugged the computer. The screen went dark.

Rodney looked like he'd just been punched in the stomach. "You say Juanita gave this to you?"

I nodded, a feeling of dread creeped over me.

"Well, then," Rodney said, "Juanita Johnson just infected our systems with a virus. That flash drive hacked our main computer."

9

THAT MEANS IT'S BAD NEWS

Rodney spent the next eighteen hours straight working on the computer. I found him asleep at his desk the next morning. He jumped when I touched his shoulder. He gave me a sleepy update, and then started working again.

Besides bringing him coffee, there wasn't anything I could help him with. I went upstairs and found Benny in our room.

"Any news from Rodney?" Benny asked.

"He finally got the virus off the mainframe," I said. "He can't find evidence that it's done any damage, but he also doesn't have his superbrain. The virus might have done something he missed. I mean, for twelve whole hours it had access to emails, files, secret identities . . . everything."

"Do you think this is Juanita's fault?" Benny asked. "Do you think the Johnsons betrayed us?"

I shook my head. "Juanita would never do that. I've just missed something. Something important."

Juanita was my friend. And besides a few hiccups here and there, the Johnsons were on our side one hundred percent. I trusted them as much as I did my own family. "Have you heard anything from her since the park?" Benny asked.

I shook my head sadly.

A knock came at our door, and Dad popped his head in. "You boys ready to go?"

"Shotgun!" Benny yelled, and raced out of the room whooping and hollering. For a second, I wished that I could forget things and move on as easily as Benny could.

It was Friday. The day we went out to the motor pool to study boring things like glove compartments and the impact of heated seats on the modern driver's mental health and well-being. Dad used to fly us out to Grandpa's ranch with his power, but now we drove. The jetpack was too risky in the daylight.

We rode in an old beat-up Mitsubishi. We could afford a really nice car—our family had plenty of money—but the older car was part of our secret identity. Plus, I think Dad had a soft spot for it.

I followed Dad, and the three of us piled into the car.

"Grandpa called me about thirty minutes ago," Dad told us as he drove. "He said he has some news and wants to talk about it when we get there."

I didn't want to ask, but I asked anyway. "Good news or bad news?"

"He didn't say," Dad answered.

Benny turned around in his seat, looking at me like he was letting me in on a secret. "That means it's bad news."

It was probably about the flash drive. This was my fault. I'd missed something.

"I feel like I'm going to throw up," I said.

"You should do it," Benny replied. "Throwing up always makes you feel better when you're sick."

"I can't just throw up on command," I said.

"Sure you can," Benny said. "Throwing up is like riding a bicycle. Except there isn't a bicycle. And you're throwing up."

*

When we arrived at the ranch, Grandpa seemed serious, almost cross. He sent Benny and me out to the motor pool to find Dirk. He and Dad stayed behind to talk.

We walked across the backyard until we came to the outhouse. Stepping inside, Benny activated the code that opened a door to a hidden elevator. We went inside, the elevator shuddered to life, and we rode deep into the belly of our headquarters.

When we stepped out of the elevator, Dirk was nowhere in sight.

Benny looked over at me, a sly smile on his face.

"Dirk's not here," he said. "Should we cross the line?"

Painted on the floor was a bright red line. All of our family's vehicles—cars, trucks, tanks, boats, helicopters—were on the other side of the line. On our side of the line were a few desks, a bookcase, and a worktable. Benny and I weren't allowed to cross the line for any reason. Dirk once said that if he was working under a car, and it fell on him, we couldn't even step over to save him. Dirk tended to be particular about his vehicles.

"If you cross the line," I said, "you'll have to deal with Dirk."

"I could outrun him," Benny said.

We both knew that was a lie. Dirk had been born without legs, but when he'd gotten his superpower—he was brilliant at building things—he'd crafted some titanium prosthetic legs with hydraulic shock absorbers. He could run faster than either of us.

Dirk stood up from behind a tank where he was working. "Of course, if you crossed the line," he said, "then I wouldn't give you the new Dirt Hog manual I just got in the mail."

That was all it took. Benny was on his best behavior until Dirk handed over the manual. I sat at a desk and tried to get into my studies, but my mind was elsewhere. When Dirk surprised us with a pop quiz, it was a welcome relief. Well, until I read the questions.

Thirty minutes later, I found myself staring at question fifty-eight.

Car horns produced on the Chevy Impala at the Oshawa, Canada, plant between 1958 and 1963 all toot in the tone of which note?
a. A♯
b. C
c. E♭
d. F

I put my pencil down, rubbed my eyes, and wished that Dirk had some shins so I could kick them.

The elevator dinged and the door opened. I turned to see Grandpa and Dad enter the room. Dad's face was pale. Grandpa looked grim. He walked straight over to me and sat on my desk. His eyes bored into mine. I wanted to look away, but couldn't.

"Did Juanita give you that flash drive, Rafter?"

I nodded. "But this isn't her fault," I said quickly. "There was something wrong. She wouldn't have—"

Grandpa held up his hands. "Nobody is accusing Juanita or the Johnsons. We're on the same side. But we're trying to re-create what happened."

I breathed a sigh of relief. I was afraid that the flash drive might cause the two families to start fighting again. And with relatives disappearing, now wasn't the time to be divided.

Dirk put down his wrench and came over. "Re-create? What's wrong?"

Grandpa's eyes never left me. "Was there anybody with Juanita?"

I looked over at Benny. He gave a slight shake of his head. "No," I said. "She was alone."

"You got there at noon?" Grandpa asked. "By the bear statue?"

"Yep," Benny said. "We got there about five minutes early. I checked my watch."

I nodded.

"What happened now?" Benny sounded worried.

"We've got two problems," Grandpa said. "Both of them serious. I just got off the phone with Rodney. The bacteria or virus or whatever was on that flash drive—it stole our passwords. Rodney just discovered that it broadcast them to a cell phone. This morning at 9:04, somebody accessed our bank accounts. The Swiss accounts, the ones in the Cayman Islands, and all of our U.S.-based accounts."

I couldn't breathe. Juanita had given me that flash drive. I had given it to Rodney and told him it was safe.

"How bad is it?" Dirk asked.

"It's gone," Grandpa said. "Our entire fortune. Everything is gone."

Somebody was making a choking sound. It was several seconds before I realized it was me.

This was all my fault.

"Rafter?" Dad asked. "Are you okay?"

I nodded my head, but it was a lie. I wasn't okay.

Nobody said anything for several moments. Then Benny cleared his throat.

"You said we have two problems?"

Grandpa nodded.

"The second problem is that Juanita's gone missing."

10

PLEASE TELL ME THEY HAVE MANUALS

"None of this makes sense," Thimon said.

This time Benny wasn't the only one pacing. I was right there with him. Thimon looked like he was watching a tennis match as his head followed us around the room.

"The day Juanita came to meet us, she left their headquarters with two relatives—an aunt and uncle," Benny said. "None of them came back."

I picked up the story. "When we saw Juanita, she was alone. But apparently, her uncle called their headquarters at ten minutes after noon and said that they were all at the bear statue, and had been since noon. We hadn't gotten there yet."

Benny continued. "But we *were* there. We were talking to her, right at noon. I know because I checked my watch and almost complimented her on her promptness. Plus, we caught the 12:33 bus afterward."

I concluded. "There is no way Juanita could have given us the flash drive. It must have been the Joneses. Somehow."

Thimon shook his head. "Do you realize what the Joneses would have to do to pull off a trick like that? You were both at the bear statue at noon. There would need to be two bear statues, and two Juanitas. The real one hanging out with her relatives, and then a fake one talking to you guys. I know the Joneses are supervillians, but they're not magicians."

"Juanita was acting strange," I said. "It wasn't her. It couldn't have been."

"What, then?" Thimon asked. "A robot? A long-lost twin? How could the Joneses have pulled it off?"

I didn't have an answer. I'd thought about it at least a dozen times on the ride home from the ranch. It couldn't have been Juanita. But it *had* been Juanita. I'd seen her with my own eyes. None of it made sense.

"I know you guys don't want to hear this," Thimon said. "But have you considered the obvious?"

"What's the obvious?" Benny stopped pacing.

"That it really was Juanita who gave you the drive."

Thimon held up his hands as both Benny and I started to talk. "What if the Johnsons made up the Joneses? What if they've been fooling us all this time? What if—"

"You're wrong." I said. "I know Juanita. I know the Johnsons. They are our friends."

"Yeah, but—"

"Rafter's right," Benny said. "The Johnsons are on our side. End of story."

Thimon looked like he wanted to say more, but both Benny and I had stopped pacing now. We faced him, staring him down. He shrugged.

"Okay, you guys have spent more time with them than I have. Just do me a favor and keep that in the back of your mind. It's a possibility."

Benny shot me a sidelong glance and gave an almost imperceptible shake of his head.

"Can we get back to the other topic?" I asked. "We've got to save Juanita. We need the powers."

Thimon shook his head. It was his turn to be firm. "Absolutely not. If Juanita really was taken by the Joneses, then the villains are up to something. We can't give away our secret now. It's more important than ever."

I was ready for this argument. I didn't want to make Thimon angry, but I had to find Juanita. She'd left her headquarters—left a safe place—because of me. *Because*

I'd asked her to. I'd do whatever was needed to help find and save her.

"Benny and I have talked," I said. "If you won't give us powers, then we think it's time to tell Dad and Mom. We need their advice."

For just a second, Thimon looked angry, and I almost took it back. Thimon was the one who gave us our powers. I didn't want to make him mad.

But then the anger was gone. Thimon rubbed his eyes. "Give me a minute to think," he said. "In fact, I'll call Uncle John and see what he says."

I nodded. "Thanks for considering it. It's important to us. Juanita's our friend."

As soon as the door to our room closed, Benny asked, "Do you think he'll let us?"

"I don't know," I said. "Let's wait and see."

Thimon came back to our room a few minutes later.

"Well, I spoke to Uncle John," he said. "I think it's time we get you guys your supersuits."

※

Benny and I stood in front of a storage unit. LL-4 was painted on the metal sliding door. On the right side of the door was a latch with a numeric keypad. I checked over my shoulder. We were alone. I took off my ski mask and Benny took off his.

"You're sure this is the right place?" I asked Thimon over my earpiece.

Benny and I had flown most of the way. When we hit the outskirts of the city, my brother insisted I put him down so he could run along the road. I heard him whooping and hollering while I soared over him in the air.

Superpowers never got old.

"Double-L four?" Thimon asked.

"Double-L four," I said. "We're standing right in front of it."

"Okay," Thimon said. "The access code is forty-five, eighty-three, four-six-five."

I typed in the code and was rewarded with a sharp click. I grabbed the handle and pulled.

Benny was inside before I could pull the door all the way up.

"You've got to be kidding me!"

It was a small storage unit. Two crates sat open against the back wall. Inside each one was a metal rod with a supersuit hanging from it.

"Uncle John sent these up," Thimon said. "He's going to send a few more sizes, just in case we need to give anybody else a power. But for now, they're all yours."

Benny had already stripped down to his underwear. I found the light switch, flipped it on, and lowered the door.

By the time I'd pulled out my supersuit, Benny was already dressed.

I pulled on my suit. It was smaller and lighter than the suits my parents and relatives wore. It was stiff and awkward until I turned it on. Then the hydraulics kicked in and everything felt smooth. I found I could move almost unhindered.

"Ah, that's much better," Thimon said.

"What do you mean?" Benny asked.

"The suits have video feed," Thimon said. "I'm picking them up on my laptop back here at the house. I can see both of you."

"Do these suits have manuals?" Benny asked. "Please tell me they have manuals."

Thimon laughed. "I don't think Uncle John sent the manuals, Benny. Sorry."

We stepped out of the storage unit. Benny started jumping up and down. The hydraulics in his suit gave him extra kick and allowed him to land softly. He could jump almost ten feet straight into the air.

I tried jumping myself, and the feeling was incredible. We had suits. We had powers. I might have been doing my superhero checklist out of order, but it was all too clear what we had to do next:

- It was time to find and defeat the Joneses.

11

I FEEL LIKE A SUITCASE

Both of the supersuits had metal handles welded to the back. The hydraulics in the suits made it easy to carry Benny around. I had flight, and Benny had enhanced sight. We'd spent the last thirty minutes flying around Split Rock looking for any signs of the Joneses.

"I feel like a suitcase," Benny grumbled as I banked left and launched us higher in the air. I still didn't want to draw attention.

I soared higher and higher. The sun warmed my supersuit. Benny groaned.

"This is high," he said. "I might be sick."

I slowed down and came to a stop. We *had* flown high.

Downtown was to our left, the rest of the city lay spread out across the valley.

"Use your sight," I said. "Look all around."

Benny fell silent. The hydraulics in his neck hissed as he slowly turned.

"With my sight, I can see almost everything," Benny said. "But there is a *lot* of everything. I don't know where to look, or even what I'm—"

Benny caught his breath.

"Do you see something?" I asked.

Benny pointed. "Fly over to the canyon, so I can get a closer look. By First Dam."

I flew over some industrial areas, then suburbs, and then I dipped down toward First Dam. The dam wasn't very large—only a few stories tall—but it held back a decent amount of water. There was enough to form a small reservoir behind it.

"There!" Benny pointed. "There's something under the water."

I had to fly closer before I could see what Benny had spotted with his enhanced sight. But sure enough, a dark object wavered under the water, right at the base of the dam.

"What is it?" I asked, coming to land at the side of the reservoir. As soon as I let go of Benny's handle, he was off and running.

"We should have packed our swimming trunks," he shouted, his voice blasting me right in my earpiece.

"Benny"—Thimon's voice crackled in my ear—"the suits have a swimming mode. Check the controls on your arm."

I scrolled through the menus of the control panel on my arm and engaged the underwater mode. The shoes of my suit extended, turning into flippers. I heard a hiss, which was followed by a cold blast of air and an increase of pressure in my helmet. Two mini propellers extended from my forearms. I knew it wasn't very cool to be impressed with your own equipment, but I couldn't help but grin. These suits were so much better than the ones my parents had.

With a splash, Benny disappeared below the water line. He kept talking over the earpiece, and his next words were urgent. "Fire! Rafter, you need to get down here as fast as you can."

I leaped into the air, flew over the reservoir, then shot into the frigid water in the middle. I kicked my feet and pointed my arms toward the black object. The propellers on my arms whirred to life and I cut through the water. It felt like I was still flying.

In an instant, I took everything in. My breathing became fast and my visor fogged up, but all my recent practice kicked in. I shoved everything else out of my mind and focused on the problem at hand.

The dark object was egg shaped, with heavy armor curving around the entire structure. It had treads beneath it, like a tank. A large drill on the front spun, boring into the dam.

Benny was already next to the robot, trying to cut into the armor with a white-hot fire. The water around him boiled and churned.

Thimon sounded in my ear. "How much water is behind the dam, and are there any houses in the area?"

My mind raced. We'd just flown over suburbs—hundreds of homes that would be destroyed if the dam broke.

"We've got to call for help." My voice sounded desperate. "Thimon, get Grandpa on the phone."

I could almost hear Thimon shaking his head. "No time. That robot is going to be through the dam before anybody can even put on their supersuit, let alone get out there. Rafter, listen to me. This isn't your chance to save the day. It's your *job* to save the day. You and Benny are the only ones who can do it. There isn't anybody else."

Juanita flashed through my mind, and for a brief moment I desperately wished she was there with us, dressed in a supersuit and fighting alongside Benny and me.

But Juanita wasn't there. She'd been kidnapped. And

right now, I couldn't think about that. I had to focus on this robot.

I took a deep breath, calming myself.

"Strength," I said to Thimon.

I heard a snap and felt a tingling. Strength coursed through my body. I dove deeper until I was right next to the machine.

The robot looked like it was built for a single purpose—to drill. There were no doors, no windows, and no hatches in the polished aluminum shell. The only way to stop the drill would be to get inside and mess up the machinery, but there was no point of entry. That meant I'd just have to make one. I pulled back a fist and pounded it into side of the robot.

Nothing happened. I'd barely dented the armor. I pounded the side of the robot again and again. I thought of the hundreds of homes—and the people in the homes—and hit even harder.

A few dents. Nothing more.

"How's it coming?" Thimon asked.

I stopped, gasping for breath. "Not good," I said. "I made a crack, but that's it. Benny? Any luck?"

Benny sounded frustrated. "No. I cut a small hole with the fire, but it'll be a half hour or more before it's big enough to get inside."

I tried to think. If I had flight, I wouldn't also have the strength to carry the robot up and out of the water. If I had strength, I'd be relying on the two propellers on my supersuit to swim. I needed more than one power at a time, and Thimon couldn't do that.

I swam to the front of the robot. The massive drill was spinning so fast the grooves of the drill appeared as a blur. Even with strength I couldn't stop it. And if the drill could cut through the cement of the dam, it would probably tear through my supersuit like it was Swiss cheese. "I've got nothing," I said. "I have no idea what to do."

"Neither do I," Thimon said.

This wasn't how it was supposed to happen. We were superheroes. We were supposed to win.

I saw Benny swimming to the surface.

"Rafter, get out of the water," he said. "I've got an idea."

"Flight," I said, swimming up. By the time I'd surfaced, I'd already felt the change. I shot into the air. Benny swam toward the shore. I dipped down, grabbed him by his handle, and carried him to the shore.

"I saw bubbles leaking out of the armor." Benny was breathing fast. "You cracked it, and I cut a hole, and now I think it's filling with water."

"Even if that's true, it's clearly still drilling. It must be waterproof on the inside."

Benny smiled. "You might want to step back."

My brother stepped to the edge of the water and submerged his fists.

"Thimon," Benny said. "I need lightning."

I realized what Benny was going to do. "Don't," I shouted. "You don't know what will—"

There was a large boom and a flash of light. A wave of energy crashed over me, and I flew backward through the air. I landed, rolled, then jumped to my feet. I raced toward Benny and helped him stand.

"Wow," Benny said. "That felt a little like kissing a tornado."

We stepped back to the water's edge, watching as the surface of the reservoir calmed. I could hear my own breath echoing inside of my helmet. I waited.

And then Benny was laughing, laughing and whooping, the water finally calm enough that we could see beneath the surface.

The robot lay on its side, the drill sticking up and no longer turning. The armor had burst from the inside, where the electricity had been conducted through the water.

Benny danced on the shore of the reservoir, his arms raised in victory.

I smiled with relief, then laughed as Benny gave me a chest bump that almost knocked me over. He whooped again and jumped into the air, his suit hydraulics making him look like he was on an invisible pogo stick.

We'd just taken on a giant underwater robot, and we'd won.

We'd done something important.

We'd saved the day.

And nobody could know a thing about it.

12

THAT SEEMS LIKE A FINE NEXT STEP TO WORLD DOMINATION

I lay on my bed, arms spread out, face to the ceiling.

Mentally, I felt exhausted. My head hurt. My brain almost buzzed with energy. Physically, I felt fine. The super-suits had done their job. Even though Benny and I had just fought with a robot, my muscles weren't tired.

As much as I wanted to turn my brain off, I forced myself to think.

"It doesn't make sense," I said.

"What do you mean?" Benny asked. "It makes perfect sense. When the two of us meet a robot, the robot is going to lose. I'm pretty much a conking ninja."

"Not that," I said. Benny must not have been tired

either, because he wouldn't stop reliving our battle. He'd been telling me about every nuance of the fight since we'd returned—like I hadn't been there and seen the battle myself.

"The robot doesn't make sense," I said. "Why was it even there?"

"Are you feeling sick?" Benny spoke like he was talking to a four-year-old. "It was there to drill into the dam. To release the water. And if the water gets out from behind the dam, that would be bad."

"But why even do it in the first place?"

Benny had an answer for that as well. "The Joneses are supervillains. It's what they do."

I shook my head. "Maybe in comic books, but not in the real world." I sat up on my bed. "Think about it. For decades, the Joneses stay in the background. They hide. They've been doing that before you and I were even born. And then they come out of hiding, kidnap the superheroes, and haul them off. Then they hide again. And suddenly their next move is to destroy the Split Rock dam?"

"That seems like a fine next step to world domination," Benny said.

"It's basic strategy," I said. "There has to be some reason they were trying to destroy that dam. And I'd bet you anything it has something to do with where they're taking Juanita and all the other heroes."

I just couldn't think of what.

I felt a swell of frustration. Juanita was my friend. She needed my help.

My head spun when I stood up. I shook it, and that helped.

"Come on," I told Benny. "We need to get back to the library."

✳

Mom and Dad didn't like the idea.

We met them coming up out of the root cellar. They were dressed in their supersuits and looked tired. When I told them we needed to leave the house for just a second, Mom put on her don't-argue-with-me face.

"Juanita went missing and she was with an adult," Mom said. "We're not going to let you two take a step outside without us."

Benny and I exchanged a glance. We'd already done a lot more than "take a step outside" today. Thimon had asked us to give him three days before we told anybody about the robot and the dam. In three days, he told us, he'd tell the family everything.

"So I take it this means you didn't find any sign of Juanita or the others?" I asked, changing the subject.

Dad shook his head. "Not a thing. And now we have another problem."

"More missing relatives?" Benny asked. He seemed

excited. Like this would give us a chance to go out and fight more supervillains.

Mom shook her head. "We haven't been doing our job, boys. We've skipped patrol and haven't been helping like we should. Today when we went out, a lot of citizens weren't too happy to see us. They feel like we've abandoned them."

Dad looked thoughtful. "We've been so busy worrying about ourselves and the Joneses, we forgot that the people of Split Rock count on us in all kinds of smaller ways. We made a mistake."

"To be honest, now more than ever we should be hunkering down," Mom said. "We have superheroes going missing left and right. There is still no sign of the Joneses. But Grandpa has spoken to Mrs. Johnson. The families have decided to get back out on patrol, starting today. It's the right thing to do."

Dad looked at Benny and me. "We'll have your supersuits in another few days. Are you boys ready to help us out?"

I thought of the supersuits that Thimon had given us. They were a better design, and with Thimon's powers, we could be more effective.

"Uh . . . sure, Dad," I said.

I used to get so excited about going out on patrol. A week ago, I would have given anything to stop hunkering down. But there was so much more happening now than my parents realized. We didn't need to patrol. We needed to take action.

✳

The next two days were the longest two days of my life. Benny spent his time reading manuals and pestering Thimon to give us powers. I spent the days doing what little research I could do from home. I looked into First Dam. I checked how much power it generated. I used an online map to find out which buildings would have been damaged if it had broken. I even read the history of when it was built.

I found nothing.

Thimon wouldn't give us powers. He said if our parents wanted us to stay inside, he wasn't going to help us disobey. "Uncle John will be here tomorrow," he said on the second day. "And then we can make our move."

That afternoon, our family supersuits were delivered in two big crates. Benny and I unboxed them. Dad said that the next morning, our family would be grouped up with two other superheroes, and we'd head out into the city to search for the missing superheroes.

After dinner that night, Thimon, Benny, and I went out back to the trampoline and watched the stars come out, one by one. I saw bats dart back and forth across the moonless sky. Their nervous energy must have been contagious.

"So, Thimon, what makes you want to be super?" Benny asked.

"That's like asking somebody why they want to be rich," I said. "Everybody wants to be super."

Benny nodded. "Just like everybody secretly wants goat's milk."

Thimon stretched out, putting his hands behind his head. Stars reflected in his eyes.

"Actually, I can tell you the exact moment when I decided I wanted to be a superhero," Thimon said. "When I was little, I got sent to the principal's office. I'd found a spilled bottle of glitter, and when I showed my teacher, she assumed I'd spilled it. I tried to explain, but I was also nervous. I'm sure I looked guilty. I couldn't even answer her questions straight. I could only shake my head when she asked me who did it because I didn't know.

"When I got to the principal's office, he was playing a card game on his computer. I remember he didn't even see me for a few minutes, and when he did see me, he looked annoyed. He kept playing his game. Maybe he hoped I'd just go away."

Benny sat up so he could watch Thimon. I tried to imagine my cool, confident cousin as a nervous little kid.

Thimon continued. "I'd never had a problem with the principal. He seemed like a nice man. But there I was. Facing what felt to me like a judge, jury, and executioner.

"Finally he turned on me. He was angry. He asked me what I had done to get sent to his office. By that point I knew I had to talk, or I'd be in big trouble. I told him I hadn't done anything. That it had all been a mistake.

"He looked at me with contempt. He sat there in his big chair, wearing his big tie. And he judged me. He didn't see the kid who'd found a bottle of overturned glitter. He saw all the other boys and girls who had been sent there before me—boys and girls who really had done something wrong. And who insisted on their innocence, just like I was doing.

"He gave me a lecture. He told me that I'd have to stay after school twice. Once for doing whatever bad thing I'd done, and once for lying about it. I tried to say something, but he slammed his fist on the table. He asked me if I wanted to stay three days after school."

Thimon didn't say anything for a moment. When he spoke again, his voice had a cold edge to it.

"I was facing a man who had all the power. I had none, and he knew it, and there wasn't a thing I could do about it. I know it seems like a little thing, but right then, I swore to myself—"

Thimon stopped, took a deep breath, and then continued. "Right then, I swore to myself that I would always stand up for those who do not have the power to stand up for themselves."

Benny nodded vigorously. I found myself nodding as well.

"That's why we need superpowers," I said. "That's why we have to do anything possible to get them back."

✳

Later that night, I lay in the black stillness of my room listening to Benny breathing deeply on the bed next to mine.

I couldn't sleep. I still felt like I was missing something. I tried to replay everything from the day Juanita went missing till now in my mind. It felt like I was doing a puzzle. I had all of the pieces, but none of them fit together. There was the mystery of Juanita's relatives. They said they'd been at the statue, but we'd *definitely* been there. How had we missed them?

And why had Juanita herself been acting so strange? When she'd looked at me, it was like she was looking *through* me. Like I wasn't there at all.

She'd given me the flash drive and then left.

I remembered the people on the bus. They had looked strange as well. Distant and empty.

Then there was the robot. We'd been threatened with giant robots and powerful lasers before, back when we used to fight with the Johnsons. There had never been any actual robots or lasers, though. They were all lies, made up by the Joneses to cause confusion. This robot was real. I'd seen it with my own eyes. That got me thinking.

If destroying the dam was so important to the Joneses—important enough to send an underwater robot—would they give up just because the robot had been defeated? Wouldn't they send another? Or maybe go and see to the job themselves?

I fumbled around on my nightstand until I found my phone. I pressed the power button and checked the time. 11:35.

I didn't want to wake Benny, so I pulled up my messenger program. Now that we'd started patrolling again, somebody would be out right now. If our computer systems were up, I could have located them immediately. As it was, I'd have to contact whoever was at the command center out at Grandpa's ranch.

I sent a message to the main number.

Anybody there? Who's out on patrol tonight?

I waited. My phone went dark after a few seconds, then flared back to life.

Isaac here. Kendal Bailey and Alisa Johnson are on patrol. They just finished downtown; now headed into the suburbs.

I thought for a moment, then typed into my phone.

May have a lead. Can they check First Dam? Make sure they check in water 2

A few moments later the answer came.

It's a slow night. I'm sure they can get on this right away.

I'd promised Thimon I wouldn't tell anybody about the

robot, and I was going to keep my promise. But if the Joneses were going to attack the dam again, I couldn't just sit back and let that happen. When the patrol got there, they'd find the broken robot, and word would spread like wildfire through the families. We wouldn't have to wait for Uncle John. Thimon would have to tell everybody about his powers tonight, and then we could use them to find Juanita right away.

I switched my phone to vibrate and closed my eyes. I should have thought of this earlier. I felt better than I had in a long time. I didn't like keeping secrets from my parents. It would be a relief not to have to hide this anymore.

✳

I woke up with a start. I didn't know how long I'd slept. Just long enough to be confused. My phone was buzzing and I could see three messages on the screen.

Nothing at the dam. Everything looks normal. They checked inside the water and the area around.

Four minutes later—**Do you want them to do anything else?**

Twelve minutes later—**Rafter, are you still there?**

The last message had come twenty minutes ago, but my phone was still buzzing. It took my sleepy brain a second to realize that somebody was calling.

I hit the answer button.

"Hello?"

The person on the other end spoke slowly and carefully.

As if the vibrations of their voice might cause an avalanche, and they were sitting at the bottom of the mountain.

I recognized the voice immediately.

It was Juanita.

"Rafter. I've escaped. I'm hiding in a linen closet and could use some help."

13

WE DON'T NEED TO THINK

I threw open my bedroom door and ran down the hall, but came to a screeching halt outside my parents' door. Benny crashed into me from behind.

It was almost midnight and they'd be asleep, but once I woke them, my parents would let Benny and me go. I knew they would. We had our supersuits now. We were part of the team.

The problem was, it would take us at least thirty minutes to mobilize. Maybe longer if they insisted on gathering everybody in the family. It would take an hour—maybe two—to get all eighty superheroes in the city to gear up and get ready for an attack.

I looked behind me. Thimon's door was also closed.

Thimon could give us powers. If I had flight, and Benny had speed, we could get to Juanita in five minutes. We could still mobilize the superheroes, but we could get there faster.

There was something else, too.

If I woke my parents, Benny and I would play a small part in a big operation. If I woke Thimon, Benny and I would be doing something big and important. All on our own.

We'd be super. We'd save the day.

We'd done it before. We could do it again.

Grabbing Benny by the bathrobe, I hauled him down to Thimon's room. I knocked lightly at the door, and when I didn't get an answer, I knocked a little louder.

"Come in." Thimon sounded sleepy.

We went in. Thimon sat up in bed. He wore a white T-shirt, and his hair stuck up at odd angles.

"Juanita's at the Baylor Hotel," I blurted out, making sure to keep my voice low. "She just called. She's escaped from the Joneses and needs our help."

Thimon threw back his covers and sprang from his bed. For a second, I thought I saw terror on his face—maybe anger—but then it was gone. He shook his head as if trying to clear his thoughts.

"Wait, start again," Thimon said. "What are you talking about?"

I told Thimon about the call I'd just gotten. "Juanita told me she was at the Baylor Hotel. She needs our help, and she needs it fast."

Thimon turned to the window. He ran his hands through his hair. "I need to call Uncle John."

"There isn't time!" The whole reason I'd come to Thimon was because he could get us to Juanita fast. "They might find her missing at any moment."

"We need powers," Benny said. "And we need them now."

"And we've got to tell my parents," I said.

Thimon turned around. "You haven't told your parents yet?"

I shook my head. "No, you can tell them after we've left. They can get the word out to the rest of the family, and we can all meet up at the Baylor Hotel."

I knew there were probably a dozen holes in the plan. I knew that my parents would want to make sure to coordinate with the Johnsons, and move with caution. But I was the one who had heard the tremor in Juanita's voice. I was the one who'd gotten her into this mess in the first place.

We had to move now.

Thimon's eyes darted back and forth between Benny and me. It appeared he was thinking fast.

"Okay, fine, you win," he said. "I'll give you powers.

We'll get you on your way, and then I'll let your parents know. We'll get them there as soon as possible. Sit down."

We sat down. Thimon touched our foreheads and I felt the familiar tingling. I felt a lightness course through my body.

I rose off the floor. I felt ready for anything.

"Fly to the storage unit," Thimon said. "Get into the suits. I'll alert the families."

✳

I stepped onto the ledge of the Wilson Tower, which stood right across from the Baylor Hotel. My toes hung over the edge of the skyscraper and my heart beat fast but steady.

Benny and I had changed into Thimon's supersuits and made it to the Baylor Hotel in under nine minutes. Thimon told us the other two families would be there in another forty-five.

Benny was bouncing around on the ledge next to me. "Let's get going," he said. "I'm ready to conk a few super-villains on the head." He smacked his fist into his open palm. Thimon had given Benny strength, and Benny couldn't wait to use it. "Man, I hope there are ninjas."

We were alone on the top of the tower. I pulled my helmet off so I could breathe the fresh night air.

I wanted to move in, but something felt off. Something had felt off ever since we left the house.

"Give me just a second," I told Benny.

The wind whipped around me, almost as if it was urging me forward. Pushing me to fly to the Baylor Hotel and start fighting supervillains.

But something held me back. Something wasn't right.

"What are you waiting for?" Thimon's voice came in my ear.

Benny looked down and whooped to the entire city. "Those people down there look like ants!"

I felt like a piece of cloth being pulled in two different directions. Close to ripping.

"Give me a second to think," I told them both.

Benny rolled his eyes. "We don't need to think. The bad guys are over there. We're superheroes. There, I just did your thinking for you."

Benny literally started to hop with anticipation. With the hydraulics in his legs, he could jump a good ten feet into the air, and he was jumping on the already high ledge of the Wilson Tower.

"Thinking is what the Johnsons do," Benny said. "We're Baileys. We do our thinking after we've already leaped into action."

Benny jumped higher and higher, the moonlight reflecting on the armor of his suit.

"Thimon, how much longer until our family gets here?"

The wind rushed and the noise of Benny jumping up and down was loud. I cupped my hand over my ear so I could hear Thimon's reply.

Thimon did reply, but I didn't hear it. Or if I did, the words didn't register.

I'd spoken to Thimon half a dozen times on the flight over here. He'd just asked me what I was waiting for.

The problem was, none of that should have been possible.

I didn't have an earpiece.

I'd never put one in.

14

A JONES

"Rafter?" Thimon's voice came in my ear. "Did you hear me?"

It was impossible.

I looked overhead and saw a full moon, high in the sky. Earlier that night, there hadn't been a moon at all.

Thoughts tumbled through my brain like cats in a dryer.

The moon in the sky.

Thimon's voice in my ear.

The flash drive that had been in my pocket, and then in my backpack.

Underwater robots and lies that were told to confuse.

Headaches.

Somebody had fooled us from the beginning.

That somebody was a Jones.

And that Jones was a Thimon.

15

WELL, NOW YOU'RE JUST BEING SILLY

"Benny," I said. "Did you put in your earpiece?"

Benny stopped hopping. He cocked his head at me. "Of course I did. Otherwise, how could I . . ." He went quiet, and then touched the side of his helmet. "No . . . I didn't. Thimon didn't give them to us this time."

The wind around us died.

"Thimon," I said. "What's going on?"

When Thimon spoke, his voice sounded somewhere between nervous and angry.

"We've been talking over the radio in your helmets," Thimon said. "Why are you two just standing around? You've got to get into that hotel."

"I'm not wearing a helmet," I said. "I took it off."

Benny took his helmet off, too, and touched his ears. His eyes grew wide. He pulled out a small black object from his ear. "Wait, I do have an earpiece. I just don't remember putting it in. Could it still be in there from the last time?"

Thimon sputtered, and then said, "Rafter, you couldn't hear me if you didn't have your earpiece. Check your ear again."

I felt my ear. Sure enough, I had an earpiece. I pulled it out, dropped it on the roof of the Wilson Tower, and smashed it under my heel.

"Guys, look at the hotel!" Thimon's voice was urgent.

I looked over at the hotel. Lights were flickering on in the top floors. I saw movement in several of the windows. Benny sucked in his breath.

"Ninjas!" he proclaimed.

Benny was right. Creeping along the hallway were several figures clothed in black. They wore masks and had swords and staves tied to their backs.

Benny looked at me with gleaming eyes. "Ninjas, Rafter! We get to fight ninjas!"

"Rafter," Thimon's voice came again in my ear. "Those earpieces are small. Sometimes they just fall deeper into your ear. You probably didn't take it out from the last time you were practicing."

Thimon was lying. My earpiece was in pieces under my boot.

I knew he was telling a lie, but what was the truth? How could I hear Thimon without an earpiece? And how could the moon be high in a sky that was dark just a half hour before?

Maybe the same way Benny and I could be at the same statue as Juanita, and still not really see her.

I know the Joneses are supervillians, but they're not magicians.

My head spun. It felt like I didn't know which way was up. My stomach lurched as the ledge seemed to shift under my feet. One moment I was watching Benny, who looked hungrily at the ninjas across the way. The next minute I was tumbling through the night sky.

"Rafter!" Benny yelled.

I still had flight. I slowed my descent and righted myself. I paused in midair, hovering between the two sky-scrapers. Benny watched me from above.

I closed my eyes. I looked at the puzzle pieces in my mind.

One by one, the pieces fell into place. A picture emerged.

The picture made me angry.

My friend was truly in trouble. She needed my help.

And I was doing nothing.

I rose back up to the ledge. I grabbed Benny by the

handle and shot into the air.

"Where are we going?" Benny shouted in surprise.

"To the dam," I growled.

"You're leaving Juanita?" Thimon sounded openly hostile now. "Rafter, why are you going to the dam?"

I said nothing. Thimon asked me the same question a second time. And then a third.

"Rafter!" Benny cried above the rushing wind. "Can you hear Thimon?"

"I can't," I lied. "My earpiece must have fallen out."

"Well, now you're just being silly." Thimon didn't sound happy.

"Everything will make sense once we get to the dam," I said. "We'll be there in three minutes."

I soared through the sky. I realized that this might very well be the last time I ever flew. I frowned, and flew on into the blackness.

I dropped down toward the mountains. The moon that shouldn't have been there sparkled on the dark water of the reservoir.

"Thimon," I said. "Give Benny fire. He's going to light up the night sky."

"Awesome," Benny said. He pointed his hands out and sprayed a giant ball of fire into the air. The reservoir lit up like a night game at the Split Rock stadium. The reflection of the light on the water made it hard to see below the surface, but not impossible. I peered into the deep water and found what I was looking for.

The last piece of the puzzle was in place.

"Do you see anything strange, Benny?" I asked. "Anything out of the ordinary?"

Benny examined the black water. He let the fire die, and looked at me over his shoulder.

"The only thing I see is the dam, the reservoir, and the Joneses' broken robot, right where we left it."

I nodded. "Exactly."

16

YOU KNOW I DON'T THINK AS FAST AS YOU

I set Benny down on the shore of the reservoir and landed next to him, the boots of my supersuit crunching in the gravel. Benny turned off his lights and my eyes adjusted to the pale glow of the moon and stars.

"Rafter." Benny looked serious. "You know I don't think as fast as you. Why are we here at the dam and not back at the Baylor fighting with ninjas and saving Juanita? Ninjas, Rafter. NINJAS!"

"It all makes sense now, Benny," I said. "When Juanita gave me the flash drive, she was acting strange. Do you remember that?"

It felt strange talking about Thimon when I knew he

was listening in, but there was nothing I could do about it.

For a brief moment, I wondered if we were in danger. But if my theory was correct, Thimon had had plenty of opportunities to hurt us before now and hadn't taken them.

Benny nodded. "Yeah, she didn't look right. She looked like she was . . . empty."

"That's a good way to describe it," I said. "The people on the bus looked the same way. I think the reason they all looked empty is because they *were* empty. Juanita wasn't really Juanita."

Benny looked excited. "You mean she was a robot?"

I shook my head. "Do you remember when she gave me the flash drive? I put it in my front pocket. But when I went to get it, it wasn't there. Thimon knew exactly where it was—in my backpack. He knew because he was the one who put it there."

"I still don't get it." Benny looked frustrated and angry.

"Two superheroes on patrol just came out here about twenty minutes ago," I said. "They looked all over the place. The robot wasn't here. Everything was normal."

My brother pulled at his hair. I could tell I was losing him.

"Benny." I tried to sound convincing. "You know how Thimon makes us sit down before and after we use the powers? And he touches our foreheads?"

Benny nodded. "To form a connection."

I shook my head. "No. It's so he can use his power. His real power. It's so he can trick our minds. He puts us in a fake, imaginary world. None of this is real. Right now, you and I are sitting in Thimon's room, in a trance. Thimon has us under his control."

17

WHAT IF YOU'RE WRONG, RAFTER?

Benny stared at me with disbelief. "How can you be sure?"

To be honest, I wasn't sure. Maybe there was another explanation, but I didn't think so. My plan was to act certain, and see if I could get Thimon to believe me.

"It's the only thing that makes sense, Benny," I said. "This is all pretend. All the times we've been trying to do something important, Thimon has been tricking us into sitting down in his room and pretending."

Benny looked around. "But, Rafter, this can't be pretend. It all feels real."

Benny did have a point. The gravel beneath our feet. The cool night breeze. The ripples on the surface of the water. It felt very real.

I stared up into the sky, as if Thimon's face might be up there, and we were in some kind of fishbowl. "It's your power, isn't it?" I shouted. "That's why Juanita seemed so strange. Because we know what Juanita looks like and sounds like, but we don't really know what she'll say. Every time we've practiced, we've done it away from others. Not just to keep our identities secret, but because making other people believable must be hard for you."

"You're both wasting time." Thimon sounded out of breath. Maybe not out of breath, but like he was moving around and talking at the same time. "Juanita needs your help back at the hotel. It's time to stop goofing off."

"You're right," I said. "It is time to stop goofing off. We spent the last three months hunkering down. And then we've spent a week with you doing nothing but pretending. Mom kept saying we were spending a lot of time in our room. That is exactly what we were doing. Sitting up in our room, not doing a thing. You Joneses are masters of misdirection and confusion. You have us fighting ourselves, then you have us hiding, and now you have us pretending to fight. You convince us we're doing something important, when in fact we're doing nothing at all."

"Juanita was right." Benny's voice was soft. "Juanita didn't hunker down. She didn't have her powers, but that didn't mean she stopped. She wasn't doing big stuff, but she was doing something. We stopped going on patrol, and she started helping other people. "

I snapped my fingers. "That's why Thimon had me beg Juanita to meet us in the park. She really did find something when she did that research. He didn't want her to find anything else. While we were pretending to meet Juanita, we were really just in our room. When she really did show up to the park, he had Joneses there waiting for her. He tricked me into getting her kidnapped."

Suddenly I was mad.

I really had gotten Juanita kidnapped. She'd managed to escape. And what had I done as soon as I found out? I'd run to Thimon. And right now, I was sitting in my room, pretending.

This had to stop, and it had to stop now.

"You are going to pay for this, Thimon," I shouted. "If it's the last thing I do."

In that moment I felt trapped. I could leap into the air and fly wherever I wanted, yet in truth, I couldn't go anywhere. I was stuck in Thimon's room.

"*Let us go!*" I shouted. I looked around, but didn't know what I was looking for. "Benny, how do we get out of here?"

"Benny, behind you!" Thimon's voice came in my ears. I realized that it wasn't in my ears like I was hearing it in an earpiece. I was hearing him as if he and I were in the same room.

Benny and I spun at the same moment. A thread of flame tore against the night sky. And then another. And a third.

"What is that?" Benny asked.

"Whatever it is, it's not real," I said. "Thimon's trying to distract us again."

Before I wasn't certain. Now I was.

I heard the familiar whine of jetpacks. The noise grew louder until three figures emerged from the darkness. Their speed slowed and they landed on the other end of the road. Their packs kicked up dust and smoke. In a moment, they had their jetpacks off and tossed to the side.

Ninjas.

Two of them drew swords. The third one had a staff. They crouched in defensive stances, waiting. I could see their eyes burning in the darkness.

"You can do this, Benny," Thimon's voice said. "These ninjas can lead us to Juanita. Beat them and save the day. Be super. Be important."

Benny looked at me. I could see the confusion on his face. "What if you're wrong, Rafter? What if this is real? We can beat these guys. If Thimon gives me speed . . ."

I looked at the ninjas. Their faces were covered. Thimon had a hard time creating other people, but a masked figure would be easier.

"Benny," I said. "This is all in our heads. We've got to break free."

Benny looked at the darkened figures. I could see his hunger to fight.

I looked up at the moon hanging impossibly in the sky.

The moon was fake. I knew it. I stared at it. Challenging it. It shouldn't be there.

Nothing happened. I stared harder, willing it to be gone.

The yellow glow of the moon seemed to shudder. I reached out my hand and took a swipe at the moon, brushing it away as if I was swatting a bee.

The moon shuddered. I swung again, and then it happened. One moment the moon was there, shining bright in a starless sky. And the next the sky seemed to dissolve. Like a football player running through a paper poster, the sky seemed to rip and tear.

I swung at the mountains and trees of the canyon, like I was clearing cobwebs from a dusty basement. I pushed with my mind. I tore at the water and the gravel and the ninjas. The ground beneath me swirled and changed. Everything seemed to shudder and fall.

One moment I was standing on gravel next to Benny in the cold night air. The next I sat on the carpet in the comfort of my home, still beside Benny.

We were alone.

My head hurt. That was why my body was never tired after training so hard with Thimon. It wasn't my body working, it was my mind.

The clock read twenty minutes past midnight. I saw that Thimon's clothes, laptop, and tablet were gone. The door to the room stood open. The stairs creaked.

Thimon was still in the house.

I jumped to my feet and took two steps to the door before I stopped. I looked back. Benny still sat on the floor, cross-legged.

He was still trapped in the other world.

"What's going on?" Benny's eyes remained closed, and he spoke in a monotone voice. "Rafter, where did you go? I can't see you."

I heard a door open. If I didn't act now, Thimon would escape. I could stop him and then come back and help Benny later.

My brain told me this was the best plan, but I couldn't do it.

I couldn't leave Benny. Not for anything.

I went to my brother and knelt down. I touched his shoulder. "Benny, you've got to wake up."

Benny's eyes remained closed, his face somber. "I want to attack the ninjas, Rafter. I want to beat all of them. This is where I belong."

"It's not real, Benny."

"I want to save people," Benny said. "I want to do important things."

I had a thought. "Do you remember your goats, Benny? You got sucked into that game, just like we got sucked into this fake world. But when something more important came along, you put the game aside. We have to do the same thing now. This is all fake. We have to set it aside."

"I'm afraid, Rafter."

That stopped me short. I almost laughed, but Benny's face was serious. "You, Benny? I've never seen you afraid in all my life. You're fearless."

Benny shook his head. His voice was almost a whisper. "I'm afraid of being a nobody."

I didn't know what to say.

Benny continued. "When I see a giant underwater robot or a Jones—and I'm afraid—I think of the fear of being a nobody. That fear is bigger than anything else. That fear pushes everything else aside, and it gives me courage."

I felt like I'd just met my brother for the first time.

"Benny . . ." I wasn't as good at speeches as Dad was. I never said some things because it made me uncomfortable. But looking at Benny with his eyes closed, I could almost imagine him asleep. "Benny, you're the best little brother a guy could want. You teach me a lot. If you'll let me, I want to teach you something this time. You and I have been searching for super all of our lives. Thimon gave us that in the pretend world, but pretending isn't enough. Not for you. Not for me."

My brother said nothing.

"Benny, Juanita is in trouble, and she needs our help. Maybe we won't be important to everybody, but we can be important to her. We're going to go out into the real world where we might get hurt. Or worse, we might try and fail. We might never be super. But either way, if we do succeed or fail, it'll be real. It'll mean something."

For a moment, Benny remained unmoving. He sat perfectly still. I didn't know what else to say.

Then he opened his eyes. I thought I saw sadness in those eyes, but I also saw determination. And maybe just a bit of anger.

"Where's Thimon?"

18

STRAGGLERS WILL HAVE TO HITCHHIKE

"Dad!" I pounded on my parents' bedroom door. "Mom, wake up!"

I heard a faint rumbling downstairs. I looked over at Benny in confusion. The noise sounded familiar, but I couldn't quite place it.

"The garage door!" Benny said.

Benny turned and raced down the stairs, his bathrobe flowing behind him like a cape. A burst of fear and excitement exploded in my chest, and I followed. Dad opened the door behind me. "What the . . . you boys know it's not Christmas, right?"

"A Jones!" I hollered over my shoulder. "Right here in the house!"

Benny ran ahead. I followed him through to the kitchen. By the time I got there, the door leading to the garage was already swinging shut. I pulled it open and raced outside.

Thimon sat behind the wheel of the Mitsubishi, backing out of the garage. His backpack and duffel bag were in the seat beside him. Benny had launched himself from the stairs and was flying through the air. He landed with a crash onto the hood of the car and grabbed the windshield wipers to keep from sliding off.

"Benny!" A moment ago I'd been focused on stopping Thimon. Now my only thought was to keep my brother safe. We weren't in a pretend world anymore.

The car backed out of the driveway, the engine whining. Thimon turned the wheel, spinning the car into the road. Benny slid along the hood but managed to hang on.

I got to the passenger side and pulled at the handle, but the door was locked.

"Benny," I hollered, "get off, you'll get run over!"

I was about to hop on the hood myself and pull Benny off when the car suddenly lurched forward and died. Everything went quiet. I could hear Dad running down the driveway. The hood of the car crinkled in protest as Benny struggled to get to his knees. Thimon cursed from inside the car.

"Stupid manual transmission!"

Benny slid off the hood but I beat him to the driver-side door, which wasn't locked. I dragged Thimon from behind the wheel, and then Benny took over. He pushed Thimon to the ground and in another second was sitting on top of him. Benny grabbed the front of Thimon's shirt and pulled until their faces were just inches apart.

"I oughta conk you on the head," Benny shouted, "for messing with my dreams and making me believe something that wasn't true!"

"Good goat gravy, what in the name of all that is super is going on out here?" Dad came to a stop next to Benny and me. "Boys, what have I told you about roughhousing in the middle of the road in your pajamas?"

"Dad," I said. "I can explain."

"Let's at least get back in the house first. It's twelve thirty in the morning!"

Benny kept an iron grip on Thimon's arms and escorted him inside. Dad managed to restart the car enough to get it back into the garage, and in a few minutes, Thimon and my entire family were seated at the kitchen table.

Dad started warming up goat's milk. I wanted to scream that there wasn't time for goat's milk, but I knew my parents wouldn't act until they'd heard the whole story.

Thimon sat down and scowled while Benny and I stumbled over each other trying to explain the events of the last two weeks. Mom had questions. Dad had questions. Even Rodney, joining us with a yawn, piped in a few times. In the end, we told them everything. The pretend powers. The flash drive that Thimon had slipped into my backpack, and most important, the call I'd gotten from Juanita just an hour ago.

"Juanita—and I assume the rest the missing relatives— are at the Baylor Hotel," I said. "The thirteenth floor. It sounds like they're in trouble."

Dad brought over six mugs, but left one of them on the tray. He looked sternly at Thimon. "I think somebody at this table hasn't earned his warm goat's milk."

Thimon rolled his eyes. "You people eat weird food. You understand that, right?"

Dad ignored him. He sipped from his mug and drummed his fingers on the table.

"Do you boys see where you made the mistake?"

"Yeah." I pointed at Thimon. "We believed that Jones over there. We never should have let him into our house. That stupid stuffed moose on his couch should have tipped us off right at the beginning."

Dad shook his head. "You got fooled, but so did the rest of us. We all did. They're supervillains who have been playing these games for decades. You've got to expect them to be good at fooling people. But that's not where you made the mistake."

I didn't want a lecture, but I figured I deserved it. And whatever mistake I'd made, I honestly didn't want to make it again.

Mom spoke up. "The mistake you boys made was not telling us. We're on the same team. We're your parents and we want the same things you do. The next time somebody offers to give you free superpowers, tell us. We might have been fooled too, but with two more sets of eyes, things may have turned out different."

Dad nodded.

"You're probably right," I admitted. "But can we have the life-lessons discussion after we stop the bad guys? Juanita needs us."

Dad threw his head back, chugging his warm goat's milk. He put the empty mug on the table with a sharp rap.

"Let me get this straight," Dad said. "You're suggesting that a handful of superheroes—without powers, mind you—just waltz into the supervillains' headquarters, find and fight a family of supervillains who very likely have their superpowers, and attempt to rescue our relatives?"

Mom clucked her tongue and shook her head.

A silence settled over the table. Benny looked confused. Mom and Dad stared at me.

"Um . . . ," I said. "Yes?"

Dad slapped the table and bellowed. "Of course yes! We're superheroes. If we don't stand up to the bad guys, then we have no right to wear our tights. I'll call Grandpa. We can have the Baileys rounded up in less than an hour."

"Don't forget the Johnsons," I said.

"Of course not," Dad said. "We work as a team. Though I have to admit, it's tempting to give our family a head start."

Benny stood up. "We get to go too, right? You're not going to leave us behind like last time?"

Dad looked over at Benny. "Do you have a supersuit?"

For a moment my heart fell. Our supersuits were fake. They were part of the lies that Thimon had told us.

And then I remembered.

"Yes," I said. "We do."

"Then go put them on." Dad grinned. "We leave for the ranch in three minutes. Stragglers will have to hitchhike."

"What about Thimon?" I asked.

Dad looked at Thimon for a moment, then made a decision. He slid the last warm goat's milk in front of him.

"Get the duct tape—we'll strap him to the Mitsubishi."

19

DO YOU BY ANY CHANCE SPEAK PORTUGUESE?

It felt like steering an ocean liner. I wanted to drive to the ranch, load up in our biggest helicopter, and fly to the hotel with guns blazing. I wanted to pull a Benny. I wanted to leap into action, and then come up with a plan in the middle of the air.

That's not how it happened. We called Grandpa and told him about the Baylor Hotel. Then everybody left to change into their supersuits.

I was the first one ready.

It's hard to describe the thrill of wearing a supersuit. You have a layer of tights that go under the armor part.

The suit itself is an engineering marvel. It's built strong to stand up to heat and blunt-force attacks. Hydraulics kick in to magnify any movement you make. The armor was bulkier than it was on the suits Thimon had us wear, but then, those were imaginary.

These were the real things.

Rodney went down to the root cellar to run the command center. If the systems had been working, he could have coordinated communications anywhere. Instead, he'd have to do it manually from the basement. The Johnsons would provide a supporting command center closer to the hotel, but Rodney would handle all the important stuff.

There wasn't anything for me to do at the moment, so I followed my older brother down to the cellar to watch him work. His fingers flew over the keyboard, and by the time I was done, he had the computer and all the communication equipment up and running.

Over the radio in my helmet, Dad told me we were still a few minutes away from leaving. I sat down on a chair, the weight of my supersuit making it creak in protest.

"I remember when you first lost your power," I said as I watched Rodney work. "You couldn't remember if a T. rex had a brain the size of a walnut or a chickpea."

Rodney smiled a half smile. "I've learned a little bit since then, but I'm nowhere near where I used to be. Sometimes it feels like I've been working nonstop."

"It shows," I said.

Six months ago, Benny and I would be popping some popcorn, sitting down here with Rodney, and watching the Baileys battle with the Johnsons. Now we were about to march into a hotel and battle real supervillains. Without any powers.

When Benny and I used to watch the battles, I'd tell him how things would be different when we got our powers. How he and I would use tactics to beat the Johnsons and win the battles.

I wondered if tactics could save us in a battle that was as lopsided as this one.

When you go up against a more powerful foe, you don't meet them head on. You hit them from the side. Or from behind. Or perhaps you don't even attack them at all, but instead find some way to—

My brain started turning. Slowly at first, and then a little faster. There wasn't much I could do right now, but there was one thing I could do for the future.

"Rodney," I said. "Do you know how the flash drive worked? How it took over our system?"

"It was actually a pretty simple script," Rodney said. "Usually a virus is complicated because it has to figure out how to get into a system. But since we just popped the drive into our computer, it didn't need anything else. The program ran through the system, copied passwords, banking information, and anything else it could find. Once it had everything, it transmitted the information wirelessly to a mobile phone."

"So if you had the code for the virus, could you modify it? Could you send the information to *your* phone?"

Rodney thought for a moment. "Yeah. That's not hard at all. I mean, all you're doing is changing a phone number. I could do that in about three minutes."

I smiled. "As it happens, that's about how long we have. Can you do it now?"

Rodney shrugged and started looking through his drawers. "Sure, but why?"

"I have an idea," I said.

✳

We were almost the last ones to the ranch. We had a long way to drive, but we also had to tape Thimon to the passenger's seat of the car. Dad, Benny, and I went inside Grandpa's house. Mom stayed behind to watch Thimon.

Baileys filled the kitchen and dining room *and* living room. A few of the Johnsons who lived in the area were also here. They'd ride with us to the Baylor to meet up with the rest of their family.

To my surprise, I saw Monroe sitting on a sofa in the living room. My first thought was to protect my ankles. Instead, I went over and sat by him.

Monroe stared at me. He looked distrustful, but not hostile. That was an improvement from the last time I'd seen him.

"Hey, Monroe," I said. "It looks like your parents told you about the family secret?"

I remembered when Dad had told Benny and me. He'd taken us camping, and told us over the orange glow of a campfire and a belly full of s'mores. It was one of my favorite memories.

"I heard Uncle Marcos talking to Grandma," Monroe said. "They told me everything after I said I knew what was going on." He hesitated. "They told me that we're all supposed to be friends now."

I smiled. "Monroe, I can honestly say that I'm glad you're on our side. My ankles are especially happy."

It appeared Monroe couldn't tell if I was joking or not. He finally said, "Nobody will let me help out. They say I'm too little."

That sounded familiar. Dad had told Benny and me about the family secret when I was ten and Benny was nine. There were a lot of things we could read and learn about being super, but we weren't allowed to do anything until we got our powers. Those three and a half years were the longest years of my life. Years of watching family members be super, but always being left behind.

"Well, you've got a lot to learn," I said. "And you've got

to get your power. Then you'll get your supersuit and you'll be ready to go on a mission."

Monroe pouted. "I can help out right now, even if I don't have a power." He pointed at two Johnsons in the hall. "Those two are fighting about which one has to babysit me. I told them I have a plan, but they won't listen."

The two Johnsons looked like they were having a heated conversation. It was clear that neither of them wanted to have to stay behind with Monroe.

I sat on the sofa, and felt like I was looking at a younger version of me. Benny and I had plans. Back in the root cellar, dreaming of how we'd save the world. Ignored or forgotten by the other superheroes. We'd felt we weren't going to be important until we had powers.

I made my voice serious. "Monroe, whichever one of those guys is lucky enough to hang out with you, you make sure to tell him your plan. And if it's a good one, then you make sure to carry out that plan. Sometimes, even the littlest things can help out in the end."

Monroe looked at me suspiciously. "Are you calling me little?"

I shook my head. "You're a superhero. Tonight the city needs us. All of us."

I left Monroe and went to find Benny and Dad.

"Why arrrrren't we alrrrready gone?" My aunt Verna

154

was saying. For months, she'd been speaking with a ridiculous English accent because she thought it was more proper. "Why arrre we just standing arrround?"

My thoughts exactly.

"The Johnsons like to have a plan," Grandpa said calmly. "Right now they're trying to figure out the best place to meet. They assured me they'll have something to us in a matter of minutes."

Nobody liked that. My family was used to leaping first, then thinking.

Finally, Grandpa got a call from Mrs. Johnson, and then announced, "We're meeting at a parking garage two blocks south of the Baylor. Everybody down to the motor pool. Dirk will assign you a ride."

Everyone got up to leave. "I hope I get to drive the Dirt Hog," Benny said.

"You know we're not driving anything," I told him. "But at least we'll finally get to ride in something."

We went out the back door and followed the group toward the secret entrance of our headquarters. "We've got to stick together, okay, Benny?" I said. "We're going up against real supervillains. This isn't going to be like fighting the Johnsons."

"We'll be fine," Benny said. "We've been practicing with Thimon, remember?"

"But all of that was pretend."

"Working together wasn't pretend," Benny said. "That part was real."

Grandpa had a huge backyard that backed up against a mountain. We got in line at an outhouse several hundred feet behind the house. It was actually the secret passage into the mountain.

I pulled out my phone. It was 1:12 in the morning. Maybe I should have been tired, but preparing to fight supervillains really gets your blood pumping.

We made our way into our headquarters and to the motor pool. Grandpa, Dirk, and Aunt Verna passed out the vehicle assignments at a small aluminum worktable in the center. Benny and I found Dad and got in line for our assignment. Two Baileys from out of town were talking about their powers.

"I used to be able to shoot whips out of my hands," a woman in her early twenties said. "But now all I can do is read someone else's mind."

"That seems like a useful power," the other Bailey said.

"Well, it's only one person's mind."

"One person at a time?"

"No. Just one person. He's Brazilian, and he only thinks in Portuguese."

"Do you by any chance speak Portuguese?"

"No."

These were the powers we were taking into battle. Somebody once said you should never bring a knife to a gunfight. We weren't even bringing knives.

More like bananas and wet wipes.

The sound of engines filled the motor pool.

"Oh, man," Benny whined. "Uncle Chambers gets the Dirt Hog. He shouldn't get the Dirt Hog. He's bald."

Machines continued to roll out of the motor pool. By the time we got up to Grandpa, there weren't many vehicles left. There were a few boats, but we couldn't exactly get to the Baylor Hotel on watercraft.

Dad stepped forward and Grandpa looked at his clipboard. "Let's see . . . Hubert. We're pretty much out of vehicles. You'll have to just take your Mitsubishi."

"What?" Benny exclaimed. "We can't show up to our first battle in the Mitsubishi!"

"Even if we did have another vehicle, you've got Thimon in your car," Grandpa said. "Nobody's staying behind and we can't just leave him here."

Benny and I had spent three months sitting behind the red line, looking at all the supervehicles we owned. I wanted to ride in one.

"What about our secret identities?" I said. "If we drive our car, somebody might figure out who we are."

"You have supersuits," Grandpa said. "No one will see you. You can rip off the license plates. I'm pretty sure the superhero code allows us to do that in an emergency."

Benny protested, but when Grandpa suggested that maybe Benny could stay behind to watch Thimon, he quickly backed down.

In a few minutes, Dad, Mom, Benny, and I were puttering down the road in our rusty car.

Thimon tried to shift in his seat but the duct tape held him fast. He was able to turn his head just enough to speak to us in the backseat. The lights of the dashboard glowed green against his skin. "Where are you taking me?"

"We're not taking you anywhere," Benny said. "Right now you're just baggage. And baggage doesn't talk."

"You're morons." Thimon smiled at me like a wolf smiles at a rabbit. "You realize there's no chance of you beating us, right?"

"When I was little . . . ," Dad began.

Benny rolled his eyes. "Here comes a story," he said under his breath.

"When I was little, I could never figure out why people wanted to climb Mount Everest. I mean, I understood people wanting to get to the top of it, but why not just take a helicopter?"

"You can't take a helicopter to the top," Thimon said. "The air is too thin for helicopters to fly."

"Exactly!" Dad sounded excited. "I never wanted to go to the top of Mount Everest when I thought it was easy.

Only when I realized it was difficult did I understand the appeal. Anybody can do the easy. The brave are drawn to the difficult."

"And the morons are drawn to the impossible."

"That's us." Dad sounded solemn. "A Mitsubishi full of morons."

"You think you've won," Thimon said. "But you haven't. That bratty girl got lucky. She called your bratty sons, and now you're all headed to your doom."

Mom stiffened in the backseat. "Well, that's not nice at all," she said. "Hubert, do you know how we found out where the Joneses are?"

"Well," Dad said. "I think Thimon got it right. Juanita escaped and—"

"It was Thimon," Mom said. "He led us right to them."

Thimon's mouth fell open. He gaped back at Mom. Even in the darkness, I could see his face turn pale. "You can't tell them that. If they think I betrayed them . . ."

Mom leaned forward in her seat. It was her turn to smile like a wolf.

"That's what happens when you mess with the Bailey family."

Thimon didn't say anything else for the rest of the trip.

20

DON'T MIND US, WE'RE JUST HERE TO SAVE THE DAY

Dad parked the car on the side of the road. He patted the pouches on his supersuit. "Does anybody have any change for the parking meter?"

"Dad," I said. "It's two o'clock in the morning. I don't think they give out tickets right now."

"That may be true," Mom said. "But we're superheroes. We always follow the law."

"We're about to break into a hotel with a bunch of assault vehicles," I said. "We drove twenty miles without license plates. We're probably going to break fifty more laws before dawn. We may as well add a parking violation into the mix."

Dad ignored me. He found a quarter in the glove compartment and dropped it into the parking meter.

"I'll borrow some money from Grandpa and feed the meter later if we haven't finished beating the Joneses by then."

Thimon snorted from the front seat, but said nothing.

Mom checked Thimon to make sure he was secure.

"All good," she said. "Up to the roof."

We crossed the street and headed to the parking garage. If we'd had our powers, Dad would have flown us to the top. Our entrance would have been a bit more heroic. But since that wasn't an option, we walked.

The parking garage was close to the Baylor Hotel, but another building blocked the view. We could set up without being spotted by the Joneses. The Johnsons had chosen the location. They were always thinking ahead.

We climbed the stairs. When I reached the top I was met by a sea of titanium, tights, and capes. Johnsons and Baileys talked, planned, and shuffled their feet nervously.

There was an electric feeling in the air. We were the underdogs going into this fight. No powers. Unsure of the numbers or powers we were about to face. We were walking right into a complex and dangerous situation, but we were superheroes.

That's what we did.

The center of attention was the Roylance's Tacos van.

That was our undercover forward command center. It looked like we were waiting for word to get the operation under way.

I didn't want to wait anymore. Nobody had heard from Juanita since she'd called me.

Benny went and stood by the side rail, looking out over the downtown area. I joined him.

"Which way is the Baylor?" Benny asked.

I pointed to the skyscraper north of us. "It's right behind that building," I said.

I looked at the reflection of the Baylor Hotel. The parking garage was tall—probably five stories—but the hotel was humongous. It had to be at least sixty stories. I craned my neck, trying to see the details in the reflection, and then realized my supersuit helmet had binoculars built in. I zoomed in and counted the number of floors. Fifty-eight stories from top to bottom.

I counted up to the thirteenth floor, but could see nothing unusual. It was possible the windows were a little darker. I couldn't be sure.

I imagined Juanita inside the building. I wondered what she was doing, and if she was safe.

"It looks like we're ready," Benny said.

We gathered in a circle around Grandpa and Mrs. Johnson. Grandpa was the first to speak.

"Okay, everybody, each family came up with a plan.

We've decided not to argue about which plan is superior."

Low murmuring broke out among the superheroes. The two families had gotten along the past three months, but this was the first time we were actually heading into a battle together. Actually, it was the first time we'd done anything major together. The families had communicated, but for the most part, each had been hunkering down on their own.

I hadn't even realized there might be some disagreement. Both families had people missing. We were on the same side.

"Since they are *both* good plans," Grandpa said in a stern voice as the murmuring got louder, "we're going to do the sensible thing. We're just going to execute both of them."

Mrs. Johnson raised her hand and the heroes fell quiet. "We will be entering the hotel in two places. One team will go directly in the front door. They will go in and up. The other team will land on the roof and go in and down. The team on the roof will need a head start since they have farther to go. We'll coordinate so that both teams arrive at the same time. We don't want to lose the element of surprise."

I had seen this kind of coordination back when my family fought the Johnsons. I'd always told Benny that we were the better fighters, but they were the better planners.

They could do more with less. We could learn a thing or two from them.

"One more thing," Grandpa said. "We're not going to divide up by families."

This time his announcement was met with full-fledged grumbling. I heard at least a couple of people spit, and thought I saw a fist being shaken. It was hard to hear Grandpa. A bunch of people started shushing the grumblers, and the noise got worse.

A sharp rapping cut through the noise. Mrs. Johnson was knocking her cane on the cement. The Johnsons immediately fell silent. The Baileys followed suit, and in a moment Mrs. Johnson could speak in a quiet voice but be heard by everybody.

"Our families have competed for far too long," Mrs. Johnson said. "If we divide up now, this whole operation will turn into a contest. We'll start fighting the Joneses, but we'll end up fighting each other. We're integrating the teams, and that is that."

I hadn't even considered this, but it was definitely strong tactics. Maybe we had a shot at winning after all. Or if not winning, at least not failing spectacularly.

"We're going to assume the worst," Grandpa said. "We're going to assume the villains have powers. But if we catch them by surprise, at least they may not have time to get in their supersuits." He held up what looked like a small pistol with a gold cylinder attached to a cone-shaped barrel. It took me a minute before I realized where I'd seen one before. It was like what my doctor used to give me the flu shot. It wasn't a barrel, but a nozzle for injecting medicine.

"These are jet injectors," Grandpa said. "You have to place them right next to the skin. One shot to the neck will cause someone to pass out in about three seconds. Our plan is to go on the offensive. Get close to the Joneses, knock them out, and then bring them to the elevators. We'll get them downstairs and in custody. The blueprints of the Baylor have been sent to everybody on their phones. Use those to navigate."

There were more questions, mostly from the Johnsons, who wanted to know every last detail. Grandpa got more and more impatient until he finally shouted, "It's time to get moving! Radio additional questions to Mrs. Johnson. She'll be running the command center here in the taco van."

Dad, Mom, and Benny were assigned to the team on the roof. I was with Grandpa on the team going in the front door. I wished Benny good luck, and he left to gather with his team.

Our team consisted of thirty-eight Baileys and Johnsons. We piled into three armored personnel carriers. The other team climbed into four helicopters. One of the

Johnsons couldn't get his seatbelt to work. Uncle Chambers couldn't find the right car, and tried to sit on a Johnson's lap. After what seemed like forever, engines roared to life and we left for the Baylor.

My stomach felt like a blizzard. I checked that the jet injector was still attached to my waist. Then I checked my radio and reviewed the supersuit's systems. I didn't know what else I should do.

The Johnson across from me had his hand resting on a crate with wheels.

"What's that?" I asked him.

"Supersuits. For the Johnsons who are being held captive. Once we break them out, we want to keep them safe. Plus, if they have their suits, they can help us fight."

There was more arguing on the trip to the hotel. The Johnsons wanted a more in-depth plan. Grandpa just kept saying the plan was to find the Joneses and stick them with the jet injector. The arguing continued until we reached the hotel.

"We're here." Grandpa kicked the back door open. "Less talking, more moving."

It was an exhilarating moment. An armored carrier. Superheroes emerging. And I wasn't watching it on the monitors back in the root cellar. Nor was I pretending with Thimon. This time it was real. This time it was actually happening.

It was terrifying and thrilling all at once.

The other armored vehicles arrived, and we combined our groups and entered the hotel. A clerk stood behind the front desk. He had a small mustache and mousy eyes. His eyes bugged out when he saw us.

"Ladies and gentlemen," he sputtered. "Uh . . . do you have a reservation? Can I help you?"

Grandpa waved his hand but never slowed down. "Don't mind us, we're just here to save the day."

The clerk picked up the phone. Grandpa took three steps, plucked the phone from his hand, and—using the hydraulics in his gloves—snapped it in two.

Grandpa looked over his shoulder. "Steven," he said—Steven was one of my cousins from Idaho—"stay down here with the clerk. We don't want him contacting anyone on the thirteenth floor."

Steven broke off from the group and stood by the clerk, who suddenly looked pale.

We got to the elevators and Grandpa pushed a button. He pulled a key from one of the pockets on his suit. When the elevator doors opened, he stepped inside, inserted the key, turned it, then hit the emergency button.

"Okay," he said. "All six elevators will be here momentarily. I suggest two people stay here and watch the front door. Rafter, you're with me."

One of the Johnsons who had been asking for more of

a plan waved his hand. "What's the plan after the elevators get here?"

Grandpa tried to look patient, but he didn't succeed. "After that, you step inside and press the button for the thirteenth floor. Six heroes in each elevator."

The elevators started to ding as the doors opened.

The Johnson asked hesitantly, "And after that?"

"After that you find a Jones and you beat on him," Grandpa said. "That's the plan."

Grandpa pushed me into an elevator with Uncle Chambers and two other Baileys. The rest of the superheroes divided up until the lobby was empty.

"Okay," Grandpa called out. "When the doors close, everybody count to three and then hit the thirteenth-floor button, got it?"

People hollered in acknowledgment.

Grandpa turned the key and the elevator doors closed.

"One . . . two . . . three," Grandpa counted. "Rafter, hit the thirteenth floor."

I turned to the elevator wall, my fingers skimming the buttons. I stopped, my hand hovering over the panel.

"Grandpa," I said. "There is no thirteenth floor."

21

IT'S SIMPLE MATHEMATICS

"Well, that's a fine fart in a furnace."

Grandpa leaned over and glared at the panel, as if staring at it long enough would make the thirteenth-floor button suddenly appear.

Outside I could hear the other elevator doors open. People sounded confused.

"Should we open the doors and adjust the plan?" I asked.

"I'm not going to stand around hoober-finching all night," Grandpa said. "The plan is the same. Hit the fourteenth floor and watch this."

I hit the fourteenth floor, and we rode in silence.

Just past the twelfth floor, Grandpa turned the key and

the elevator jerked to a stop.

Grandpa pulled at the doors. The hydraulics in his supersuit hissed and the doors screeched open.

A solid metal wall stood in our way.

"Confound tarnation," Grandpa spat. He turned the key and hit the fourteenth floor. The elevator rose, dinged, and we stepped out into an empty hall.

Uncle Chambers pointed to a door with a sign reading STAIRS. We went through the door into a stairwell. We went down a flight of stairs, but there wasn't a door that let us back into the building. Clearly there was space for a thirteenth floor, but we couldn't get to it.

We heard footsteps above us. The second team came into view. Dad and Benny were with them.

"Weren't you taking the elevators?" Dad said.

"No elevator access to the thirteenth floor," Grandpa said.

We went back to the landing where the thirteenth floor should have been. Two Johnsons were there, checking for a hidden door.

"Could we break through?" Dad asked.

The wall was made of solid concrete.

"Maybe," Grandpa said. "But it would take too much time, and we'd likely lose the element of surprise. They'd hear us beating on the wall."

"Where's Mom?" I asked Benny.

"There are four stairwells," he replied. "She's in another corner of the building."

I checked my phone. It had been more than two hours since I'd gotten the call from Juanita.

Grandpa took control again. "Hubert, you go back to the roof. See if there is some other way to the thirteenth floor. We'll go back down and see if the little guy at the front desk can do anything else besides wipe his own nose."

My phone beeped. So did everybody else's in the stairwell.

I pulled my phone out, a feeling of dread growing in my stomach. The message on my screen was from Juanita's grandmother, back in the taco van.

Juanita is in IMMEDIATE danger. Get to the thirteenth floor at all costs.

While I was reading the first text, a second text appeared, this one just to me.

Please save my granddaughter.

That was all it took.

Several things happened at once. The Johnsons started talking, fast and furious, discussing best options. Grandpa pushed everyone standing next to the wall to the side, and started pounding on the concrete with his armored fist. Chips of rock and dust flew out from the wall. If Grandpa had his power, he would have been through that wall in a matter of minutes. But even with the enhanced supersuit, it was going to be slow.

The Johnsons, apparently having reached a plan, headed down the stairs. Dad moved next to Grandpa and started attacking the wall too. They worked in perfect concert, each hitting the same place in the concrete, but at different times.

Benny looked to me. "What do we do, Rafter? I don't want to just stand here."

There wasn't room at the wall to try to help break through. My brain raced. "Dad," I said. "Call us if you get through."

Dad paused his attack. He looked at Benny and me. I knew he wanted to tell us to stay close. To stay with him so he could watch over us.

But that isn't what superheroes did.

He nodded. "Stay safe. And keep in contact over the radio. If *anything* happens, you call for backup, is that understood?"

I grinned and nodded. I pointed up the stairs. Benny didn't need any other encouragement. He turned and led the way. We went up several floors and then took the elevator the rest of the way to the top. I followed Benny to the door that opened onto the roof.

"What next?" Benny asked.

I didn't know what next. I looked around the roof, taking

in the situation, listing in my mind anything that might help. There was some window-washing equipment, several large ventilation systems, a few doors leading to what looked like small sheds, and our helicopters.

I ran to the edge of the roof and looked down.

There was clearly a thirteenth floor, which meant that there had to be a way to get people and things onto that floor. We could lower the window-washing equipment to the thirteenth floor, but the glass was probably strong. It would take a massive force to break through.

"Come on, Rafter," Benny urged. "Juanita is in trouble."

My breathing became rapid, and my chest felt tight. Benny was right. We needed to get onto the thirteenth floor, and we needed to do it now.

Juanita was in trouble, and friends are there for each other. No matter what.

I put my fingers against my temples and cleared my brain. The time for careful, thought-out planning was over. I needed an idea, even if it was completely crazy. We needed to leap into action.

Leap.

Leap. Jump. Fly.

My brain delivered an idea that was, in fact, completely crazy. So crazy it probably wouldn't work.

But if it did work, it would be *awesome*.

"Benny," I said. "You've read the manuals. Do you think

there is any possible way you could drive the Dirt Hog?"

Benny's eyes bugged out. He looked like he'd just won a beauty pageant. His face lit up and he started dancing around me.

"Yes! Yes! Rafter, I totally can. I promise. Whatever you need. I can do it."

I opened up a communication channel limited to Benny and Dirk. "Dirk, this is Rafter. Do you read me? Where are you?"

Dirk's voice came in my ear. It reminded me of Thimon talking "through our earpieces," but this time everything was real.

"In the lobby. We're trying to find somebody who will give us access to the thirteenth floor, but so far no luck. I think we're wasting our time."

"Can you fly us back to the parking garage in the helicopter?" I asked. "I have an idea."

∗

I tied the steel cable to the Dirt Hog. We'd cut the cable from the window-washing machinery.

"What exactly are we doing?" Dirk asked. He sat in the helicopter, watching Benny and me. One end of the cable was tied to the skid of the helicopter, and the other end was tied to the motorcycle.

I took a deep breath. "Benny, fire up the Dirt Hog."

I heard two shouts. One was Benny shouting in

excitement as he jumped on the motorcycle. The other was Dirk, shouting in horror.

"You can't drive the Dirt Hog, Benny!" Dirk cried. "You've never done it before. You don't have your license. And nobody's even shown you how it works."

"Maybe not," Benny said. "But I've read the manual."

He kicked his right leg and the Dirt Hog roared to life.

I checked the knot one more time. That knot had to hold. I mean . . . it really had to hold.

I climbed onto the bike behind Benny. "You're sure you can drive this thing?"

I could tell he was grinning by the way he talked. "To be honest, I have no idea, but we're about to find out."

"I'm starting to think this is a really, really, bad idea," Dirk said in my ear.

"We're ready, Dirk," I said. "This is the plan. We need you to lift us off the parking garage with the helicopter. Then lower us to the ground. From there, Benny is going to drive toward the hotel. You fly above us." That wasn't the whole plan, but it was enough to get started.

It was all Benny needed. With a twist of his wrist the vehicle roared even louder. He shouted over the motor. "I've read a lot of things about how to work a clutch, but the whole thing is still fuzzy in my brain! You might want to hold on. Tight."

It was a good thing Benny gave me the warning or I'd

have ended up on the concrete. I wrapped my hydraulic-enhanced arms around his waist.

The Dirt Hog roared and jerked at the same time. The front end of the motorcycle rose into the air and the bike lunged forward. We shimmied from side to side and I was certain we were about to crash, but then the front wheel landed on the ground and we straightened out. Benny opened the throttle and we tore across the front of the parking lot.

"Fly, fly, fly!" I yelled into my microphone. I was talking to Dirk, but Benny thought I was talking to him and gunned the bike, racing even faster.

I had the sudden image of Benny and me dragging the helicopter across the roof of the parking garage, or else being flung from the bike as the cable went tight and the helicopter yanked us back.

But Dirk was already on the move. The helicopter roared and climbed into the air.

"Where am I going?" Benny asked. "I could use some direction."

He seemed awfully calm for somebody who was already doing forty miles per hour across the top of a four-story parking garage, headed for a three-foot wall.

"Pull us up," I yelled into the radio. "Lift us over that wall!"

The helicopter blades sliced through the air. The cable

was long, the helicopter was high, and the wind tore around us like rushing water. Dust flew everywhere. I watched two things with complete and total concentration: the wall racing toward us at a frightening speed, and the cable, snaking up into the air.

"Hang on!" I yelled as the cable went tight. I locked my arms around Benny, who held on to the motorcycle with his hydraulic gloves. The bike rose into the air and lurched sickeningly to the left as Dirk banked toward the hotel. As soon as we were over the wall, Dirk dropped the helicopter.

In another moment we were on the ground. Benny gunned the engine and straightened the motorcycle out like he'd done this every day of his life. After a few wobbles, we were racing down the road toward the hotel, the cable still attached to the helicopter but no longer tight.

Benny whooped in elation. I whooped, too, although I think my whoop sounded more like a scream of terror and relief.

The cable had held, but now came the hard part.

"You two are crazy, you know that?" Dirk's voice sounded at once angry and impressed.

"Why, thank you," Benny said.

"Rafter, you have about ninety seconds before we get to the hotel," Dirk said. "If you're going to tell us your plan, you'd better do it fast."

I was glad I only had ninety seconds. Dirk wasn't going

to like it and I didn't want to give him time to argue.

Taking a deep breath, I opened my mouth to explain. Something caught the corner of my eye.

I whipped my head around. For a split second I was certain I was seeing things.

Stepping down from a bus was Monroe Johnson. He was followed by the Johnson who had been assigned as his babysitter. And behind them walked three other figures, all in bathrobes. One of them had a walker.

Merry, Judith, and Barbara from the senior-citizen center.

Whatever plan Monroe had, it involved waking up three former superheroes and hauling them down to the Baylor Hotel.

I didn't have time to give a second thought to Monroe. I hoped his babysitter and the ladies would all stay safe.

I had more pressing concerns. The hotel was getting closer and closer with every passing second.

I shouted into my radio. "Okay, this may sound a little crazy, but we're going to drive the Dirt Hog into the hotel. Right through the windows."

"Honestly, that doesn't sound any crazier than leaping from the top of a parking garage," Dirk said. "The Dirt Hog's armor should crash right through the glass front doors. But why—"

"That's good to hear," I said. "But we're not aiming for

the front doors. We're going to crash through the windows . . . on the thirteenth floor."

Benny swerved to miss a car, gunned the engine, and continued to drive toward the hotel. I could hear the sounds of the city, the roar of the Dirt Hog, and the chopping of the helicopter, but no one said anything for half a block.

And then there was screaming.

Benny screamed that it was the best idea he'd ever heard. Dirk screamed at us to pull the Dirt Hog over and park it right now.

"Listen!" I screamed back. "There isn't any time to argue. Benny, your job is to drive at the hotel as fast as you can."

Even as I said it, Benny opened the throttle, causing the bike to pop a wheelie. I held on tight and the hotel loomed in front of us as we raced forward.

"Dirk," I said. "You have to fly the helicopter up so that we crash through the thirteenth floor."

"That's impossible," Dirk shouted. "If I'm off by even a few feet you'll be smashed against the side of the Baylor."

We only had a few more seconds.

"It's not impossible," I said. "It's simple mathematics. As soon as we leave the ground, you check the altitude of the helicopter. Each floor of a building is ten feet, right? Just fly up a hundred thirty feet, and that will put us through the windows on the thirteenth floor."

Dirk would tell me later that it wasn't anywhere near that simple. But I'd said something that convinced him. *It's simple mathematics.* In fact, it was extremely complicated geometry. But Dirk knew numbers. Even without his power, he could do this problem on the fly—*literally.*

Dirk was one of many heroes that night. He did several things at once, and in an incredibly short amount of time. He pushed the helicopter forward and up. As soon as the cable went tight, he noted his altitude.

Then he pulled out his phone. While Benny and I hung on to the Dirt Hog for dear life, Dirk looked at the blueprints of the Baylor Hotel. He found out that the main floor was in fact nineteen feet, and all the other floors were each twelve feet, eight inches.

As soon as he had this, the rest was simple.

He gunned the engines, flew the helicopter forward, and slammed Benny and me into the thirteenth floor of the Baylor Hotel.

22

YEEEEEEEEHAAAAAW

Dirk's aim was true.

The nose of the Dirt Hog crashed through the window. The armored metal struck the glass, and the window exploded into a thousand sparkling bits. Time seemed to slow down.

Benny and I sailed through a pastel-colored hotel room. I caught images as I flew. Two beds. A minifridge. A TV sitting on top of a dresser. A painting of an Italian village on the wall.

Everything glittered from the pebbles of glass that filled the space in the room. Benny had let go of the Dirt Hog and flew, fists out, through the air.

He was screaming *yeeeeeeehaaaaw*.

I was upside down.

Time returned to regular speed. The Dirt Hog smashed against the far wall and crashed to the floor. Benny slammed into a coffee table and then bounced off a couch. I flew through a doorway, struck a shower, rebounded off the tile, and then crushed a toilet.

As soon as I'd stopped moving, I hollered to my brother. "Benny! Benny, are you okay?"

I heard a groan, and then the hiss of hydraulics. Benny's voice came from the main room. "I am *totally* changing my middle name to Dirt Hog. I'm not even joking."

I breathed a sigh of relief, and then went about checking everywhere I hurt.

The supersuits had saved us. They were built for protection. The suits kept our arms and legs and heads from bending the wrong way. They kept the glass from cutting us. They kept our heads attached to our bodies, which I appreciated very much.

I crawled to my feet, white porcelain crunching under my boots. My head was spinning and my heart was beating fast, but other than that, I felt fine. Much better than one could reasonably expect to feel after flying a quarter mile through the air and being sling-shot into a skyscraper.

The helicopter still flew outside. I ran to the Dirt Hog and untied the cable. I tossed the cable out of the gaping hole in the side of the hotel, and waved to let Dirk know we were okay. He saluted us, and then the helicopter rose into the night sky.

I turned and found Benny brushing off his supersuit. He looked at me, a broad grin on his face.

"We did it, right, Rafter?" he said. "We rode a Dirt Hog through the air. We crashed through the window and survived. We're heroes, right? We're super, just like last time!"

I could see elation in his eyes.

I'm afraid of being a nobody.

I had to tell him the truth.

"Not yet, Benny," I said, and Benny's face fell. "Anybody can drive a Dirt Hog through the thirteenth floor of a hotel. Well . . . anybody who is crazy or not very bright. But that doesn't make us heroes. Not just yet. Juanita had it right. We hunkered down, but she helped others. Maybe it didn't look heroic, but it was. And now it's our turn. Let's find some people to help. Then we'll be heroes."

Benny thought about that, and then nodded. "Point me in the right direction, and tell me what to do."

It took me a second to determine what that direction was. To be honest, I was surprised that nobody had found us yet. Crashing through the window had caused quite a bit of noise.

I opened a channel to Mrs. Johnson. "Are you still in contact with Juanita?" I asked. "Do you have her location?"

She must have been busy coordinating other things

because it took a moment for her to answer me. When she spoke, it was quick and no nonsense. "She's hiding in the linen closet on the thirteenth floor. Southeast corner."

"Southeast," I said, pointing. "That's the right direction."

I looked out the peephole of the door. I saw figures racing past. Men and women, most of them in pajamas, but some of them in hotel-staff uniforms. A few times, I thought I saw a flash of metal. If it was what I thought it was, these people were Joneses.

I didn't know if the noise from the Dirt Hog had awoken everybody, or if they were already running around before we got there. Either way, it looked like we'd caught them by surprise.

We had to move fast.

My brain raced. I remembered my promise to Dad. *If anything happens, call for backup.*

"Hey!" Benny had the door to the minifridge open. "Chocolate milk!"

"No time for chocolate milk," I said. "It's time to move."

Benny quickly joined my side.

"This is the plan," I explained. "Juanita is out this door and to the left. There are a bunch of supervillains out there. None of them are in supersuits, but they probably have powers."

Benny looked grim, but nodded.

"The elevators are also to the left. When we go past them, press the buttons. Both up and down."

"I like to press the buttons," Benny said. "What do we do after we get Juanita?"

I hadn't thought that far ahead. Maybe because I didn't think we'd even make it that far. "I have no idea."

I turned on my radio and opened a channel to everybody.

"This is Rafter and Benny Bailey. We're on the thirteenth floor, and we're going to call the elevators to us. If anybody is in the lobby, please get in and ride up with them. We could use the help."

I knew there were going to be a thousand questions. Maybe my family would even tell me to stop, and wait for them.

But Juanita was in trouble.

So I threw open the door to the hotel room and ran.

23

DID YOU HIT YOUR HEAD ON THE WAY HERE?

The Joneses were in a panic. Men and women ran down the hall, everyone trying to get . . . somewhere. I couldn't tell if people were running for their supersuits, trying to escape, or if it was just chaos.

But at the sight of me and Benny in our supersuits, the chaos intensified. Joneses shouted. They ducked out of the way, or into hotel rooms.

We ran.

I lowered my shoulder like I was running with a football. Nobody tried to stop us.

We paused at the elevators just long enough for Benny

to push the buttons. Hopefully my family had had time to get in the elevators below.

Then we were running again. I waited for an explosion of fire. A bolt of electricity. Or somebody with strength to step in and stop us.

No one did. And so we kept running.

At the end of the hall was a door labeled LAUNDRY. It was locked.

Benny took three steps back, then ran and hit the door with a crash. The frame splintered and the hinges gave way. The door ended up on the floor.

The room was empty. Cupboards held bath towels, hand towels, and washrags. Several large laundry bins on wheels held dirty laundry, along with hand soap and bottles of shampoo and conditioner. A sink rested against one wall of the room. A clock hung on the wall.

"Juanita?" I said. "It's me, Rafter."

There weren't many places to hide, but as soon as I said her name, one of the laundry bins exploded. Dirty linen shot up and out like lava from a volcano. Juanita pushed herself out of the bin and tossed a towel that was stuck on her head to the floor.

"It's about time you guys got here." She tried to sound stern, but she was too clearly relieved. "Where's everybody else?"

"It's just us for now," Benny said. "Everyone else is try-ing to figure out how to get up here."

Juanita looked like she wanted to ask more questions, but I knew we didn't have much time. So far nobody had followed us into the linen closet, but I expected that to change any minute.

"Where are the rest of the missing relatives? Are they here in the hotel?" I asked.

Juanita nodded. "They are in rooms 1301 to 1305. Also, as far as I can tell, none of the Joneses have real powers. Their powers are all worthless, just like ours. And there are about fifty Joneses altogether."

It took me a moment to fully grasp what this meant.

That's why nobody stopped us running down the hall. They had dud powers, too. We had more people, *and* we had supersuits.

✳

A moment ago it had felt like we were on a doomed mis-sion, but we'd been given a miracle—we were superheroes charging a castle expecting to fight dragons, but finding only cute little puppies. We were going to win.

"Juanita," I said. "Do you want us to get you to safety?"

Juanita looked at me like I had a gopher crawling out of my ear.

"Did you hit your head on the way here?" she asked.

She sounded offended. "Why in the world would I want to get to safety?"

I looked at Benny for help. He shrugged.

"I didn't think you wanted to be a superhero," I said. "You know, you were doing things like helping out at the senior center and stuff."

Juanita reached over and knocked on my helmet. "Uh, hello. I love being a superhero. I just didn't want to be a superhero that sat around and did nothing. If I couldn't do something big, I was at least going to do *something*."

"Now you're talking," Benny said. He reached out and knocked on my helmet too. I guess because he thought it looked fun.

"My mom was a superhero," Juanita said. "And I am too. Big or small, I'll help where I can." Juanita looked shy for just a second. Then she pushed me gently on the shoulder. "Get me up to speed. What's happening downstairs?"

I told Juanita what had happened. I even told her quickly about Thimon and how he'd tricked us.

I heard the elevator ding. I backed up to the door and peered around the corner. There were fewer Joneses in the hall now. Doors were slamming. I heard another ding and held my breath.

Johnsons and Baileys started pouring out into the hall.

Grandpa led the charge. He hollered orders to those

following him. I radioed the room numbers Juanita had given me. In a moment we'd gone from being alone on the thirteenth floor to being surrounded by superheroes racing to save the day.

Even if the suits looked a little similar, you could easily tell who were Baileys and who were Johnsons. The Baileys were already kicking in doors, shouldering their way into rooms, and generally shouting and crashing around. All of them held jet injectors. Some of them held two.

The Johnsons, on the other hand, worked together. They'd taken just a moment to plan, and now explored rooms methodically in two and threes.

One of the Johnsons spotted us. He pointed toward the elevator. "Juanita, your supersuit is over by the elevator." Juanita ran to get it.

Dad spotted me. "Rafter, can you keep shuttling up superheroes? The battle is already under way, and I don't want to miss any of it."

"Aw, man," Benny whined. "We're going to get stuck chauffeuring superheroes." He watched the action in the hall hungrily. "We're the ones who got everybody up here—can't we do the fun stuff?"

I felt the same way, but I liked to think I'd learned a few things.

"Sometimes we get to do the big stuff," I said. "And sometimes we need to do the small stuff. Come on, we can move fast, and maybe there will still be some villains to capture."

We passed Juanita racing back to the linen closet to change. We started bringing heroes up the elevators. By the time we had everybody up on the thirteenth floor, a few superheroes were already bringing Joneses over to be sent down. The jet injectors must have worked fine because the unconscious Joneses looked like they were taking Sunday afternoon naps.

These supervillains had evaded us for decades, but now I could see them, and they looked like regular people, especially when they were asleep.

Well, regular except for the fact that every one of them had a metal plate attached to their head. That explained the flashes of metal I'd seen earlier. The plates were the size of a medium pancake, and were molded to their skulls. Many of the men were bald, and the women had hair growing around the metal. It was beyond creepy, but at least it was an easy way to keep track of who the bad guys were.

A man in pajamas turned the corner. He didn't have a metal plate. He carried a supervillain.

"Uncle Buford!" I said. "We found you!"

Uncle Buford gave me a thumbs-up. "Worst shopping trip ever! But I like how it's ending."

Uncle Buford turned and left.

"If we don't get out of here," Benny said, "they're going

to ask us to shuttle the bad guys downstairs."

"What should we do?" I asked.

Juanita turned the corner right as I asked the question. She was dressed in her supersuit.

"I don't know what you guys are going to do, but I am going after October Jones. This time, he doesn't get away."

24

I DEFINITELY THINK WE SHOULD USE OUR ANGRY VOICES

Juanita led us down the crowded hall. I had a flashback to just a few months earlier, when she'd led us effortlessly through the dump.

On the way, she explained how she'd escaped from her hotel room. She'd left the shower running and then hid under the bed. When the maids came to change the sheets, she'd snuck into the laundry bin.

"I thought I'd escape as soon as the maid left me alone, but she never did," Juanita said. "The maids might be in on it."

"Supervillain maids?" Benny said, dodging a pillow that a Jones had just flung at a Johnson. "Not as cool as ninjas, but still kind of awesome."

"Lucky for me there was a service phone in the linen closet," Juanita said. "That's how I called you, Rafter."

"If the maid never left you alone," I asked, "how do you know where October is hiding?"

"When I was in the bin, everything looked normal except for this one door at the end of the hall. Even the maid seemed afraid of it."

In almost every room, and spilling out into the halls, Johnsons and Baileys were wrestling with, throwing things at, and all-in-all tangling up Joneses. It wasn't much of a fight. With their supersuits, the heroes could overpower the villains almost effortlessly. Still, none of the villains used powers.

Grandpa walked down the hall, a big grin spreading out under his mustache. He carried two unconscious Joneses, one over each shoulder.

"Now we're cooking with gas!" he proclaimed as he walked by us.

Benny whacked me on the shoulder. "Hey, we know that guy." He pointed to one of the Joneses Grandpa was carrying.

At first I didn't recognize him, but then I saw it. "Charles!" I said. Charles was the guy we'd fought at the cell-phone tower back when we'd met October the first time.

We got to the end of the hall. Juanita turned the corner

and pointed to a door with a sign that read JANITORIAL SUP-PLIES.

"Wait a minute." Benny sounded excited. "There aren't really any janitorial supplies behind that door, are there? What's back there? A ray gun? A death machine?"

Juanita shrugged. "I don't know what's behind there. But think about it. All of the rooms we've seen make up only half of the hotel—the south side. There's another whole side to floor thirteen, and this is the only door that leads to it—at least that I could find. If October Jones is anywhere, I'd bet it's in there."

That was all Benny needed. He stepped forward, lifted an armored leg, and slammed it against the door.

He went flying backward, crashing against the far wall and crumpling in a heap on the floor.

"What the . . . ," Benny said, getting to his feet. "That worked on the other door."

"This door must be reinforced," I said. "Somebody wants to keep us out."

"Benny." Juanita tried to hide a smile. "Have you ever heard of Newton's third law of motion?"

Benny strode toward the door. "Unless that law says *at some point the door has to break*, I'm not interested. All I have to do is kick harder."

"Wait," I said. "Juanita has a point. If you kick harder, you'll just go flying back harder. You need more weight."

Benny looked confused. "You want me to gain weight? Like . . . right now? You're the one who never lets me drink chocolate milk."

Juanita rolled her eyes, but I thought I saw a smile in there somewhere. "It's amazing you guys could find me at all. Benny, stand here and give me your elbows."

Benny stood facing the door. Juanita backed up against him and locked her elbows with his. She crouched down and dug her heels into the carpet. I guessed what she was doing, and went to place my hands against Benny's back. I straightened my legs, bracing myself.

It was a little awkward. Juanita and I were almost nose-to-nose. It almost felt like a hug.

"Uh . . ." Benny sounded uncertain. "What are you guys doing back there?"

"Just kick, Benny." I said. "Sir Isaac Newton and his laws say this might work."

Benny didn't do things halfway. With his elbows locked with Juanita's, he lifted both feet up off the floor and cocked them against his chest. Juanita supported his weight easily. I braced my feet and waited.

Benny kicked.

Hard.

I felt the force of the impact through my suit, its frame shuddering beneath the blow.

Everything held. Well, everything but the door. The door flew off its hinges, breaking into pieces and skittering across the floor.

"Kapow!" Benny cried. "I like that Newton guy. Does he have any other laws?"

"He wrote a whole book," I said. "Like a manual for the real world. You might like it."

Light from the hall lit up the first few steps past the door, but beyond that was only darkness. Juanita stepped carefully through the doorway, touching a panel on her wrist. I did the same, flipping on the infrared in my helmet. Blackness turned to a ghostly green.

"Wait," I whispered. "Benny, we're doing exactly what we did last time. We're going off and doing something on our own."

"Don't tell me you're backing out! We can totally handle this on our own," Benny said.

"Maybe we can," I said. "But it's always better with friends."

I looked at Juanita, who stared at me for a moment, and then nodded.

I flipped on my radio. "Mom, Dad, I think we've found October. End of the hall. We could use some backup."

There was a pause, and then I heard my Dad's voice. "Confirmed. Anybody not fighting Joneses, get to Rafter."

Mom's voice was next. "On my way."

Knowing the superheroes would join us soon, we stepped through the door into darkness.

✳

Instead of another hallway with rooms, the other side of floor thirteen was one gigantic room—the size of a small warehouse.

The place was a mess. There were workbenches and half-built—or half-torn-apart—vehicles and supersuits and other machines I didn't recognize. A dirty rug lay on the floor next to a few couches and chairs. I couldn't tell if people really hung out or even slept here, or if this was just where they threw away their old garbage. Clothes and trash and blankets littered the floor.

Then I spotted them: computers, stacked on top of one another in racks. Back to plan A.

I pulled the flash drive out of my pocket and stepped over to the computer rack. I plugged the drive into the biggest machine. I had no idea if this was going to work. It had always been a long shot.

"Rafter!" Juanita whispered, but I heard her voice loud and clear through the radio. "Over there." In the middle of the warehouse—with his back toward us—sat a thin figure. He sat in front of a large bank of monitors, his shoulders slumped.

I couldn't see his face, but I knew at once who it was.

The thin frame. The bald head with a metal plate attached.

October Jones.

I heard footsteps behind me. Johnsons and Baileys began to file into the room. I smiled. This time we weren't going up against October on our own. This time we had a family—make that *two* families—of superheroes.

Juanita inched forward in the darkness, toward October. From where I stood, I could make out what was on the monitors. They were feeds from security cameras, just like we had in our basement. Each monitor showed a similar scene.

Johnsons and Baileys beating Joneses.

October must have seen this. He must have realized his defeat. It was our moment of victory. Good had prevailed, as good always did.

October sat, watching his empire crumble around him. In that moment, I almost felt bad for him. I knew what it felt like to have your dreams taken away.

Benny's voice was the faintest whisper in my radio. "What should we say, everybody? We need a really good line. Something like . . . 'You've finally met your match, buster.' Is *buster* a swear word? I don't want to swear, but I definitely think we should use our angry voices."

I didn't have a chance to answer. No one did. In that moment October swiveled in his chair to face us.

I will never forget the look on his face. He turned and

faced two dozen superheroes, but his look wasn't one of despair or defeat or grief. It was a grin. A horrible, wicked, toothy grin.

"Hello, Rafter Hans Bailey," October Jones said. "I've been expecting you."

25

IT'S A TRAP!

Benny clenched his fists, the tiny motors in his supersuit whirring and clicking. Juanita crouched, ready for anything.

I stood with them, focused on October Jones. When a supervillain says he's been expecting you, it's best you sit up and pay attention.

He wore a supersuit. His head was bald. His face thin and leathery. I know I'd seen him once before at our encounter at the dump, but he looked familiar in some other way. Like I'd seen him more recently.

October stood. He took a step toward us, and then another. His voice was cold and raspy. "Well, if it isn't my favorite trio of idiots."

"Your mom is a trio of idiots," Benny said.

Mom's voice came from behind me. "You're surrounded, October. And the rest of your family has been taken. It's over."

October ignored her. "Juanita, I must thank you. Poor Thimon was terrified when you told everybody where our headquarters were. But look, now you're all here. In one place. It's really worked out quite well."

A sudden realization hit me. I lifted up my hand so that half of October's face was blocked. Just like the bandage that had covered his face in Three Forks.

"You pretended to be Uncle John!" I shouted.

October laughed. "Pretended to be Uncle John? If you'd bothered to look into your ridiculous genealogy, you'd realize that you don't even have an Uncle John. You Baileys are so gullible."

Half of the superheroes behind me growled.

I should have guessed it earlier. That's why Thimon kept calling Uncle John. He was asking October what to do next.

"Enough small talk." October finally addressed the rest of the people in the room. "I must thank you all for gathering together. It will make the next steps much easier."

Juanita leaped forward, her fist pulled back ready to strike. October raised a hand and Juanita lifted into the air. She kicked with her feet, but was otherwise immobile.

Benny ran forward, along with three other super-heroes, but October lifted them all into the air.

"Come now, Juanita," October said. "Just because you didn't see any Joneses with powers, you assumed that we were all powerless?" He *tsked* his tongue. "I must admit I'm disappointed. I expected such gullibility from the boys, but not from you."

October had his powers. That meant that the rest of the Joneses . . .

I looked at the monitor. There were still several fights going on. Dad had one Jones backed into the corner of a hotel room. I called through my radio, "Dad, it's a trap! The Joneses still have their powers."

A few of the superheroes in the room turned to go help the others.

October rolled his eyes. "Have you really not figured it out? Have you never asked why we don't simply get rid of your family? Why we go to all the pain of capturing you?"

October reached up and knocked on the metal plate atop his skull. "And have you never wondered why we all appear to have chrome domes?"

I didn't say anything. I had wondered about those things, but I knew firsthand how impossible it was to find answers on the Joneses.

Dad's voice sounded in my ear. He was breathing hard.

"If they have their powers, they sure didn't put up much of a fight. I think we're just about finished out here."

It was a trap. I just didn't know what kind.

"We're not collecting superheroes," October said. "We're collecting powers."

He waved his hand, and I felt my stomach sink as I rose up several inches off the ground. "This power here? It's courtesy of your old friend Charles. He wasn't making good use of his power, letting three children defeat him, so now it's mine. It's much more useful in the hands of a genius."

October lifted both hands. I heard cries behind me. All of the superheroes now hovered in the air.

"I was the one who made the breakthrough," October said. "We'd been studying powers for years. My metal-plate technology was the first breakthrough in transferring powers, but we found the brain wouldn't let go of a power unless you tricked it. Replaced the real power with a worthless one. I tried it out on my own blood first, and it worked well—the metal plates were just a little messy. Finally, I figured out how to make the technology digital, and I just had to try it on you idiots."

"You mean the other Joneses—" I started to say.

"Oh, yes, Rafter Hans Bailey. All of the Joneses out there in the halls have a worthless power, just like you. As long as they live, their real powers are right here"—he tapped on his head—"with me, October Jones, Super-super. That is why I need all of you alive. Your powers are worth more to me than the satisfaction of saying good-bye to you forever."

October smiled that wicked, horrible smile. "Imagine an army of Super-supers. We'll be using the power of the very people who are supposed to stop us. It's deliciously ironic."

October's hand glowed blue. Benny floated toward October Jones.

"You," October said, pointing at Mom. "Get on your radio and tell everybody in both your families I want them in this room in three minutes. If anyone tries to escape or stay behind, the little boy pays for it."

"I'm not little," Benny scowled.

"Let my son go." I'd never heard Mom so angry. Her voice was cold.

One of the Johnsons spoke up. "You can't threaten children. We'll work with you, but let the boy go."

October threw out his hand. Lightning flashed, arcing toward the Johnson and cutting a scorch mark in the wall above his head.

"Now!" he shouted.

There was nothing any of us could do. October had Benny.

Mom explained the situation on the radio. Aunt Verna ran to the elevators and called them up to the thirteenth floor, one at a time. Group by group, the room filled up with superheroes.

As I watched them file in, something caught the corner of my eye. Across the room, in the computer, the flash drive blinked green.

My heart beat fast, like I'd just sprinted the length of a football field. I was sweating under my helmet, and I had the sudden desire to pull it off and breathe in fresh air. I tried to calm my panting but nothing helped. I only felt like I needed more air.

October's voice sounded smug. "I think we're missing somebody. Not everyone who was invited to this party has arrived."

I looked around the room. I couldn't see anybody who was missing. Even Juanita's grandmother and the two Baileys who were with her in the taco truck were here. All of the superheroes were in one place, under the control of October Jones.

The door to the warehouse flew open. A figure walked through the door. He had bits of duct tape stuck to his shirt and arms, but he had a smirk on his pinched face.

Thimon Jones.

26

WELL, THAT WAS EASY

Thimon strode into the room, cocky and cruel. It was clear that if Benny could break free from October's grasp, he would have made up for not conking him earlier.

As it was, we were all helpless. If we did anything, October would hurt Benny.

"Well, that was easy." Thimon walked directly toward me. "I have to admit, Uncle October, I was hoping for a bit more of a challenge."

Thimon stopped, his nose a few inches from mine. He picked a piece of tape from his shirt and stuck it to my helmet.

The worst thing I could do was lose my temper. I focused on slowing my breathing.

"You superheroes are so predictable," Thimon said. "So easily distracted. It's the simplest thing to keep you from doing your job. From doing something—anything— worthwhile."

My face grew hot. I breathed in through my nose, and out through my mouth. I counted three breaths before Thimon spoke again.

"You know that story of me and my principal? And the horrible, horrible case of the spilled glitter? That was all true. The best lies are mostly truth. When my principal punished me for something I hadn't done, I made a promise. Not a promise to stand up for those who are powerless. A promise to destroy those who have power."

Thimon had fooled me completely. I saw hate in his eyes that I hadn't seen before.

"No more," Thimon growled. "We're about to give the world a wonderful gift. A world without superheroes. We'll be the ones in control. Nobody will have power over us."

October ordered the families to stand in lines. He pushed Benny over against the far windows, still hanging in midair. If we tried anything, October would have no problem throwing him outside, or finding some other way to hurt him.

Thimon and October spoke in hushed tones. Then, Thimon turned to face us. "All right, everybody take off your helmets. I don't need to remind you what will happen to the little guy if you don't obey."

"Will people please stop calling me little?" Benny yelled.

Dad stepped forward. "Let Benny go. Take me hostage. Or any of us. Even you wouldn't hurt—"

October whirled on my father. His voice was twisted with anger. Spittle flew from his mouth when he spoke. "Do not make the mistake of assuming what I would or would not do. Your children have powers, and that makes them valuable to me. But they also made me look a fool last time I met them. It would not take much to convince me to make sure that they never get the opportunity to do that again."

Dad must have seen something in October's eyes. He took off his helmet and stepped back in line.

One by one, the superheroes took off their helmets. The Joneses already knew our secret identity, but it became apparent what they had planned. Thimon walked around to each Bailey and Johnson, touching each of them on the forehead.

He was making mental connections. He'd told Benny and me that he could only give powers to the two of us at once, but apparently he'd been lying about that, too.

Thimon touched my forehead. I scowled at him. Sweat trickled down my neck.

After Thimon was done, October put his hands behind

his back, and walked in front of the superheroes. He spoke like a drill sergeant speaking to new recruits.

"All right, this is what we're going to do. Any deviations, and bad things will happen to Benny, am I understood?"

I heard a faint buzzing. It took me a minute to realize that somebody was calling me on the radio.

I took a chance and, as soon as October and Thimon were turned, put my helmet back on.

"Rafter, are you there? Rafter, come in."

It was Rodney.

"What is it?" I whispered the words so that only Rodney could hear. October was talking and waving his hands in the air.

"Rafter, it worked." Rodney's voice was filled with excitement. No, not just with excitement—with exuberance. It sounded like he might be dancing with pure joy. Except that he couldn't be dancing, because it sounded like he was driving. I could hear an engine in the background, and the noise of cars driving past him.

"What worked?" I whispered.

"The flash drive," Rodney said. "It worked just like you thought. It infiltrated the Joneses' computer system and sent everything to me back at home. I have it all, Rafter. I have *everything*."

"I'm very happy for you." I didn't bother hiding my despair. "But have you been listening to the radio? October has us all captured. It doesn't matter if we get our money back. He's won."

"Money?" Rodney said. "What are you talking about?"

"The money October stole from us," I whispered. "You said it worked. Did you get it back?"

"Oh, that," Rodney said. "I didn't even try to get our money back. I mean, I guess I can later, but that isn't what I was after."

"Rodney," I said. "I'm a little busy, can you get to the point?" He reminded me of the old Rodney. The one who was so incredibly smart, but didn't understand how to say what he meant. Sometimes it was so bad that—

I stopped in midthought. It couldn't be. It was too much to hope for.

"I stole their code," Rodney said. "I plugged it into the device, and it worked. The device worked. I have my powers back."

I took a sharp breath, and when Rodney spoke again, they were the words I wanted to hear.

"If you can hang tight for a few minutes, I can give you back your power. I can give everybody back their powers."

27

OR 20.3 KILOMETERS, IF YOU PREFER METRIC

October Jones had stopped his little speech. I hadn't heard a word he'd said, but I knew what I had to do next.

I had to stall.

October Jones strode back in my direction. He'd said earlier that we were more valuable alive than dead, but I didn't like the look on his face.

I had a thousand questions for Rodney, but one question was more important than any other right then.

"How much longer till you get here?" I whispered.

"Oh, I don't have to actually be there," Rodney said. "I just have to be within a certain range. Specifically, twelve-point-six miles. Or twenty-point-three kilometers, if you prefer metric."

I managed not to scream at Rodney. Barely.

"I'm already on my way. By my estimations, I'll be there in six minutes and fourteen seconds. If the Burlington Avenue light is green, I can shave off eighteen seconds. I'm certain on that time. Man, it's great to have my ability back. All this brainpower!"

"What are you doing, Rafter Hans Bailey?"

October stood before me. He had one of the jet injectors in his hand.

"Oh, nothing," I said, scrambling to take off my helmet before he figured out what I'd done. I hoped that Rodney had the good sense to stop talking. I counted down in my head: *six minutes left.*

October held the injector out to me, and I took it from him.

"Ummm . . . ," I said. "What am I supposed to do with this?"

October's face darkened. "Have you not listened to a single word I've said?" he screamed.

I thought about zapping October with the jet injector, but he likely had superspeed.

October leaned in until I could see the thin bloodlines in his eyes. His voice was quiet and icy and smelled of cheese. "You humiliated me the last time we met, Rafter. I told you that I wouldn't forget. This is the first of a hundred different ways I'm going to get my revenge. I need your family unconscious so that we can shave their heads and perform a little brain surgery on them. You, my dear boy, are going to help me."

Five minutes left.

Stall.

"What if I refuse?" I asked October.

"Well, I could hurt you," October said. "And believe me, that would bring me great pleasure. But right now it would be more effective if I hurt somebody you care about."

October reached out a hand. Benny moved away from the window a few feet, and then slammed against it. The window held, but a large crack spiderwebbed out from the center.

That scared me. For a moment I thought about abandoning my plan to stall. To yell for Rodney to stay away. Anything to keep Benny safe.

Benny shook his head, a defiant look on his face.

I remembered Benny's words. *I'm afraid of being a nobody.* Benny wasn't afraid of October, so I wouldn't be either.

"Okay," I said. "I'll do it."

I checked the jet injector to make sure it was loaded.

I clicked the safety on, and then off. Anything to stall for time without looking like I was stalling for time.

I started in the back row. A Johnson stood before me, his gaze steady. He didn't look afraid.

"I'm sorry about this." I winked. I held the gun to his neck, tilted it just a little, and pulled the trigger. I saw a spritz of moisture fly out behind the man's neck.

For a moment the Johnson did nothing. He stood there looking confused, and I worried that everything would be ruined. Then I saw understanding in his eyes. The Johnson crumpled to my feet and sprawled out on the floor.

I took a breath and stepped to the next superhero.

I looked over my shoulder. "You won't get away with this," I said to October. Then I repeated the same procedure with the next superhero. I pretended to inject her, and she collapsed to the ground.

October laughed. "Oh, I won't? And tell me, Rafter, who is going to stop me? You? By this time tomorrow, you'll have a metal hat, and I'll have your power. You'll be like a regular citizen, only worse. You'll be a failed superhero."

I pretended to zap the next hero, and the next. Each of them fell to the ground. All it would take was one hero to miss the fact that they should be pretending, and October would realize what I was doing.

Two minutes, thirty seconds.

"Speed it up, Bailey." October called from the front of the room. "Finish the job or your little brother will be checking out of this hotel permanently." Benny bumped lightly against the glass.

When I got to Juanita, she gave me a nod. She looked ready for a fight, but pretended like the others, falling to the floor.

I stepped toward Dad. He'd seen what I was doing. He looked nervous. None of the others knew that Rodney was on his way. That in a few moments, they would have their powers.

It's okay, I mouthed.

Before I could inject Dad, he spoke up. "October Jones, you're a horrible human being. You don't hold children hostage."

I went through the motions and Dad fell to the floor, but October laughed. "A horrible human being? Humans are alive today because they are good at surviving. By bending the world to their will. Controlling those around them. If anything gets in our way, we push it aside, or enslave it, or destroy it. Humans are masters of control and strength and destruction. That makes me better at being human than anyone else in this room."

October stopped talking. He looked over at me, waiting for me to continue. I was too close. Almost all the superheroes were on the ground, and those left standing were directly in front of October. He would see I wasn't injecting them.

Forty-five seconds.

I took a breath.

"You're wrong."

October glared at me. He raised a glowing blue fist to remind me that he was still in control. "What did you say, little boy?"

"I said you're wrong." I took a step toward October. "Humans *are* good at a lot of things. Control. Enslavement. The ability to hurt and kill. We're good at all of those things."

I dropped the jet injector and took another step. "But humans are good at other things too. Hope. Love. Helping those who have fallen."

I took another step. October looked at me with disdain, but said nothing. I was close enough to touch him.

I heard sirens in the distance. I hoped Rodney had called the police. If October noticed, he didn't show it. But he was listening. I saw Benny lower to the ground.

"There are two kinds of humans," I said. "Those who hurt and destroy, and those who help and build. When people like you commit your ugly acts, a thousand others step in and show the world what it really means to be human."

I felt anger grow inside of me. I didn't care what October

thought. I looked him right in the eye.

"And you forgot one crucial thing."

"What's that?" October sneered.

"There are more of us than there are of you."

I felt a surge of energy, and my true superpower surged through my bones.

28

HE'S GOING TO ESCAPE

Strength flowed through muscle and bone. I felt the familiar sense of gaining a power and knowing everything about it.

I stepped back, jamming my helmet back on, flexing my hands into fists.

I grinned at October Jones. I was ready for a fight.

Benny's eyes went wide. I nodded, and then he was gone. There was a burst of air and he was by my side. I heard the clanking of metal and the hiss of hydraulics as a company of superheroes—fire on the tips of their fingers, lightning crackling between fists—stood and faced October Jones.

Baileys. Johnsons. All of us together.

October's eyes went wide, then became narrow slits.

I imagined what must have been going through his head. He could fight. He might even have a shot at surviving—he was, after all, a Super-super. Each of us only had one power, and he could find our weaknesses and destroy us, one by one.

But he didn't want to destroy us. He wanted our powers.

And together we were mighty.

Fury crossed October's face. He looked at the super-heroes behind me, and then his eyes rested on mine.

I knew I'd never forget that look.

He opened his mouth and made a sound. A primal cry of anger, frustration, and defeat. The cry became a bellow and he raised his hand. A wall of flame burst toward me. I bent over, covering my face, shielding myself from the heat.

"Thimon, deal with this!"

The flash was a distraction. When I looked up, October had disappeared.

Invisibility.

At that precise moment, the room erupted.

The door burst open, and Joneses in supersuits came rushing through. Water, wind, fire, lava, and lightning blasted from outstretched hands. Several Joneses flew through the air, another smashed through the wall, opening another entrance for a second wave of supervillains.

The wall of windows shattered behind us. Joneses on ropes swung into the room. Helicopter blades tore through the night, and spotlights shone in through the shattered windows.

It was absolute chaos.

Everybody started shouting at once. Grandpa tried barking orders through the radio but they were hard to hear and there was no time to group up. With the flame and water and lightning arcing through the air, it was all anybody could do just to stay on their feet.

In a matter of seconds, full-scale battle raged through the room.

My heart raced. I felt a moment of panic and looked around to see who needed help.

All around me, the fighting had become immediately intense. Grandpa took on three villains at once. My dad was flying through the air, picking up villains and tossing them to the side of the room. My mom's hands glowed blue as she pushed villains around with her power.

Baileys and Johnsons were jumping, diving, throwing punches, kicking the feet out from under the villains. Everywhere we were winning. Nobody was getting hurt. Nobody was losing. And yet more villains poured in through the doors and the windows, as if there was an endless supply.

The fighting was amazing. The battle epic. It was unbelievable.

Because it was all fake.

Thimon had touched each of us on the forehead. He had made a connection, and right now, we were all fighting our imaginations.

"This isn't real!" I shouted into the radio. "This isn't real. The villains aren't real!"

No one heard me. There was too much going on—too many people shouting over the radio—for anyone to pause.

Besides, they were all living their dreams. They were being super. They were beating the villains and nobody was getting hurt. They were doing something they thought was important.

I focused on a villain. I swung my arms, willing him to be gone, just as I'd willed the moon out of the sky and the dam and forest to be gone.

The villain vanished. I focused, and tore through the fake battle, banishing the imaginary scene from my mind. Villains began to disappear. The windows became whole again. The warehouse suddenly became quieter. The villains disappeared. I watched my relatives and friends dance and lurch around the room, still fighting imaginary foes.

I found Benny. He was thrashing around in a small area. It looked like he was fighting a half dozen Joneses. He moved with closed eyes.

I opened up a direct communication with him over the radio. "Benny," I said. "Benny, can you hear me?"

"Yes!" he replied. "Isn't this amazing? Isn't it . . ." Benny stopped moving. "Carn sarn it. This isn't real, is it?"

"No," I said. "It's not. Can you break free from Thimon's control? Remember the goats."

It took Benny a moment, but then he had his eyes open. He looked around the room, his face angry. "That's twice he's tricked me. Where is that guy? I'm doing a lot more than conking him on the head."

I hadn't thought to look for Thimon, but he either had invisibility, or he could control us at a distance. Both he and October were gone.

We found Juanita against the wall by the windows. She was attempting to take down imaginary helicopters, trying to stop the rush of villains into the room.

It took us a good three minutes to explain what was going on, and then walk Juanita through breaking the connection on her own. Benny and I had already done it once, so it was easier. Juanita finally opened her eyes.

She was as angry as Benny.

I turned back to the room where the rest of the superheroes fought imaginary foes. "We're going to have to help each one of them break the spell, one by one."

Juanita shook her head. "We can't," she said. "Either October is trying to get away, or he's getting ready for another attack. We need to find him. Now."

"It will be easier if we have help," I said.

"But by the time we break the connection, October will be gone."

"We don't even know where he went," I said. "How do we—"

"There!" Benny pointed.

A helicopter careened into view, about four blocks away. It was headed straight for us.

"It's another fake," I said. "Thimon is still trying to get into our minds."

I willed the helicopter out of the sky. I tore at it with my hands.

Nothing happened.

"The roof!" Benny and Juanita said at the same time. They both turned and ran toward the door.

I took one last look at my family, still trapped in the grip of Thimon's power. I didn't want to leave them, but Juanita was right. We had to stop October, no matter what he was planning.

I turned and followed them.

"Rodney!" I cried into the radio. "The device worked! How much longer till you get here?"

"There are three variables in my route," Rodney said. "The light at Riverside and Fielding, the merge at Hammond Street, and then there is the whole pedestrian situation at—"

"An estimate!" I shouted. "All I need is an estimate!" I caught up with Benny and Juanita just as the elevator doors opened. I stepped around the unconscious Joneses and got in the elevator.

"Two minutes, twenty-eight seconds, plus or minus forty-two seconds."

Benny pushed the button for the roof. The doors closed and we began to rise.

"Everybody is still under Thimon's control. You'll have to break them out of it. Talk to them, explain it's not real, and they can break the connection."

"Roger that," Rodney said. "Where are the rest of the Joneses?"

"You don't need to worry about them."

"Wrong, little brother," Rodney said. "That's exactly where we need to focus. October doesn't have our powers anymore, but he still has his family's. If some of our Shockers can short-circuit all the metal plates, October Jones will be powerless."

The elevator seemed to take forever.

Benny started hopping from one foot to the other, like he had to use the restroom really bad.

"He's going to escape!" he said. "We can't let him, not this time."

"He's not going to escape." Juanita's voice was firm.

I put myself in October's shoes. He was invisible, so he could have gone anywhere. Why wait for a helicopter when he had the power to fly?

Of course, there was Thimon. Thimon would likely need a helicopter. Or maybe the helicopter wasn't for escaping. Maybe it was bringing somebody.

We were getting close to the roof. I stepped forward in the elevator, flexing my fists. I could feel the strength in my muscles. I felt like a caged tiger, ready to pounce. Benny crouched next to me, preparing to run. Juanita lifted her hands, flicks of flame dancing on her fingers.

The elevator dinged and came to a stop.

29

AT LEAST I GOT TO CONK A JONES

The doors opened. Outside, the helicopter roared. It hovered ten feet from the roof and dipped toward a landing pad. A radio tower stood dangerously close, and the helicopter kept having to swerve to avoid it.

I saw the reflection of blue and red flashing lights on nearby skyscrapers. The police had arrived and parked in front of the skyscraper.

Thimon stood near the pad, his eyes still closed in intense concentration. October stood next to him. I could see his mouth moving, but whether he was talking to Thimon or into his radio, I wasn't sure.

Either way, he didn't look like a man running away. He looked like a general issuing orders to his troops. He looked like a villain preparing to fight back.

Juanita and Benny acted first. Juanita took three steps and knelt, and flame streaked out of her hands. The fire shot out like water from a hose, lighting the entire roof in an explosive orange glow. I tucked my face into the crook of my elbow and waited until the heat rolled over me.

The helicopter retreated higher. Whoever was flying the craft was smart enough to avoid a ball of fire.

Benny disappeared in a burst of speed, reappearing to wrestle Thimon to the ground.

"Stop messing with my brain!" he hollered. He made a fist and conked Thimon on the head, just enough to make a point.

Benny was only a few feet from October Jones—a Super-super.

I raced forward. As I ran, I heard the noise on the radio as it changed from elation to confusion. I realized what had happened. Benny's tackle had broken Thimon's concentration. The rest of the heroes were free.

"Dad," I called on the radio as I ran. "Send any Shockers to the unconscious Joneses, Rodney will tell them what to do. Send everybody else up here. October is on the roof."

There was still confusion, but Dad started issuing orders.

The cavalry was on its way.

The hydraulic drives in my legs and feet whirred as my

legs pumped. The added boost allowed me to run faster than normal. My power helped me to run faster still.

But it wasn't fast enough.

October Jones had his fist in the air. It glowed blue, and in a moment Benny was floating above October's head. I skidded to a stop.

"Put my brother down!" My voice roared over the chopping of the helicopter blades.

"You brats don't know when to quit, do you?"

October held out his other hand, and I felt my stomach lurch as I rose off the ground. Juanita joined me, and in another moment Benny was at our side. The three of us clumped together in the air.

October glared at us. "I know how to handle superheroes who don't quit. I regret having to destroy three powers, but I won't regret destroying you."

He reared back, like he was throwing a baseball. I tried to grab on to something—anything—but October had me too high in the air.

"At least I got to conk a Jones on the head," Benny muttered.

October flung his hand, and in a flash we were hurtling through the air. The cityscape lurched in my field of vision, and I had a sickening sense of vertigo. We were careening over the roof, higher and higher.

And then we were falling. The invisible hand that had

pushed us suddenly was gone. I landed with a thud on the roof, and was able to keep from falling off the side. Benny fell, but rolled to his feet in a flash. Juanita landed like a cat.

October stood on the roof, confusion and anger on his face. He stared at his hands, and then held them back out at us.

Nothing happened. He'd lost the power to move things with his mind. Downstairs, my relatives must have started short-circuiting the metal plates.

October began rising into the air himself, then thought better of it and landed again on the roof. He wouldn't want to lose his power while flying over the city.

The helicopter above us dipped again, narrowly missing the radio tower. It gave me an idea. I ran to the base of the tower and pushed. My muscles strained. I dug my feet in and felt the metal bend under my force.

The tower began to tilt. I aimed it just right, and with a final push, the tower came crashing down on the helicopter pad. Now the helicopter had no place to land.

October held his ground. He eyes darted around, as if he was trying to determine his next move. And then he turned and charged at the three of us.

He skidded to a stop, landing on a foot and one knee. His hand came up, and I saw lightning crackling between his fingers. He snarled and threw his fist directly at me, like he was throwing a punch even though there was still twenty feet between us. His eyes almost glowed with the reflection of snapping energy.

My arch nemesis had attacked. For three months I'd planned out how I would fight October when I saw him again. But in the end, I did nothing.

I froze.

Benny didn't.

One instant I was looking at a ball of lightning. The next instant I was on my side, the air knocked out of me. Benny had pushed me aside, and was already scrambling off.

"Sorry, big brother," Benny said. "Hope that didn't hurt."

Juanita put up a wall of flame between us and October. "Get behind something!" she yelled. "Move!"

Juanita was already racing. I saw a bolt of lightning fly through the fire and strike where Juanita had been. Then a second bolt, and a third. October was firing blind.

Benny had disappeared as soon as Juanita yelled. I ran behind some metal piping and Juanita scrambled behind a large fan. A wall of water extinguished Juanita's flame with the sound of a wave breaking. The night became dark once again.

If October still had water, there wasn't much Juanita could do with her flame.

The elevator dinged. October spun. There was a crash

of thunder and a flash of light as October threw lighnting at the door.

My heart dropped. "Is everybody okay?" I held my breath.

"We're okay," Grandpa's voice came over the radio. "But the elevator door is welded shut. We're going to have to go back down and take the stairs. We'll be another two or three minutes."

I didn't know if we could hold off October for two more minutes.

Juanita stepped out from behind the fan. Fire roared from her hands, but no sooner had she started than October lifted one arm and extinguished her flame with a second wave of water.

Now lightning crackled from both fists. October grinned, his teeth flashing in the darkness, his eyes wide and filled with hate.

There was a rush of wind and October's back arched as Benny hit him from behind. October and Benny landed in a pile of arms and legs. Benny pulled himself away from October, and then almost immediately he was standing next to me. He was panting and grinning.

"We've got to get this guy," he said. "What's the plan?"

I looked around the corner of the pipes. October saw the movement and spun on his heels. His eyes were filled with hate and fury. He threw out his fist at me but nothing happened.

He was losing more powers.

October let out a scream. He glared at me, and then called over his shoulder. "Thimon! We're leaving."

Thimon had retreated next to a shed on the far side of the roof. Now, he stepped out of the shadows.

"Split us up," October said.

Thimon closed his eyes.

30

THAT'S REALLY STARTING TO FROST MY CUPCAKE

I wasn't prepared for what happened next. October Jones stood there, a look of defiance on his face.

And then a second October Jones stepped *out of* the first one. This October raced for the broken elevator. Before I could move, a third October peeled away and ran toward a ledge. There was a roar in the air as six helicopters suddenly flew from behind neighboring skyscrapers and came toward us.

More Octobers stepped out of the others—I could no longer tell which was the original one. Some ran toward the helicopters, some ran to different ledges. Two of the Octobers stepped forward as if to attack.

"He's messing with our brains again!" Benny screamed. "That's really starting to frost my cupcake."

I saw multiple Thimons start to run as well. In just a few seconds, we had twenty or thirty supervillains—all of them copies of either October or Thimon—running around the roof.

"Find the real October!" I shouted.

The three of us leaped into action. I brushed aside two Octobers who were stepping forward to attack. I willed them away and they faded into the darkness.

One October was almost to the elevator. I reached out with my mind and he disappeared.

"Where is he?" Juanita shouted. "Which one?"

Benny was the quickest. He ran from October to October, from Thimon to Thimon, swinging his fists, trying to find the real villains.

I kept track of the villains who were almost out of sight. The October who was on the ledge, ready to jump. The Thimon who was slipping behind some pipes. As soon as I determined they weren't the real ones, I'd look for more.

I heard a sharp metal clang and suddenly Benny was flying backward out of a large shed.

"Found him!" Benny yelled, even as he skidded across the roof and slammed into a ledge. He pointed toward the shed and groaned. "He's in there."

I ignored all the other Octobers and Thimons. We could

track down Thimon later. But October Jones could not get away. I raced toward the shed. The door was still open, but I couldn't see anything in the darkness.

Just as I got there, October emerged from the shadows with a crossbow in his hands. He lifted one foot and kicked me in the chest, his boot clunking against the armor of my supersuit.

I had only a split second to brace myself, and use my power to keep from flying across the roof. But the blow was still powerful. I stumbled back, bumping into Juanita, who had come up from behind to help me. Our legs became entangled and we both went sprawling to the ground.

October made it to the ledge. He aimed his crossbow and shot. I heard a high-pitched whirring sound, and then a clatter. But he hadn't been aiming at us. As I got to my feet, I could see a thin cable disappearing into the darkness. One end was connected to something in the shed. October had shot the other end to a neighboring skyscraper. He pulled at the cable, testing its weight.

We had all the exits blocked, but by sliding across the cable, October could escape.

I wasn't going to let that happen.

October Jones pulled a tether with metal clips on each end. He connected one clip to the ring on his harness, and the other end to the cable. He turned to look at me, his eyes cold and piercing.

"Before this night is over, Rafter Hans Bailey, you will see my face again. It will be the last thing you ever see."

He stepped off the roof of the Baylor, and slid away into darkness.

31

YOU WOULDN'T HURT ME

We moved as a team.

Benny, of course, was the first to react. He had speed, after all.

He was also craziest.

He ran straight to where October had the cable secured, and when he ran out of building he just jumped. The super-suit gave him good lift, and the speed gave him incredible distance. I moved to the ledge. I watched in fear and amaze-ment as Benny soared into the air. For a split second I thought it was the last time I'd ever see my brother.

He arced wildly through the night sky. Just as he began his descent, he came into contact with the far end of the cable. He reached out with two hydraulically strengthened gloves, grabbed hold, and came to a stop. The cable bounced and dipped, but held.

October skidded to a halt in the middle of the cable. Benny waited for him at the other end.

I wanted to hug my brother right then and there.

October looked back toward us. Juanita let loose a burst of flame, as if to convince October that coming this way wouldn't be any better than going toward Benny.

There was nowhere to go. We had him trapped.

"You've been beaten!" Juanita shouted. "We have the rest of the Joneses. Give up now and you won't get hurt."

"You wouldn't hurt me." October's voice cut through the darkness. "That's the difference between me and you. You are weak and I am strong. I'm willing to do whatever it takes to get ahead."

October Jones reached down and pulled a wicked-looking knife from a sheath attached to his leg. Hand over hand, he began to move toward Benny.

No one threatened my little brother.

There was no time to think. No time to plan.

I crouched, leaned forward, and jumped into the blackness.

32

I BEAT YOU AGAIN

I soared through the darkness. My suit had given me a good boost, but most of my speed came from my own strength. My superpower. I'd coiled my legs like giant springs, and then exploded forward. October had only a fraction of a second to respond, and luckily it wasn't long enough.

I slammed into the villain, wrapped my arms around him, and kept going.

I heard the harness snap and October gasp as the wind was knocked out of him. Then the two of us were tumbling through the night sky.

I grabbed the knife from October, bent it against my titanium suit, and then dropped it.

"You've lost, October," I growled. "I beat you again."

If October was scared, I couldn't see it on his face. I saw only pure hatred.

"You've killed us both, you stupid boy."

October was right. The Baylor was fifty-eight stories tall. That meant we had about six seconds before we hit the ground. I knew my suit would shatter under the blow, and even my strength wouldn't be enough. I could survive a three- or four-story drop, but not much more.

I felt surprisingly calm. My family was safe. Benny and Juanita were safe.

That was all that mattered.

33

GOTCHA

A hero never acts alone.

For every hero you see on television or read about in the newspaper, there are other, unmentioned heroes who helped.

I didn't save the day. I helped save the day.

It took Juanita half a second to see what I was doing. Another half second and she'd jumped after me.

My power gave me a boost. I was traveling fast. But Juanita had flame. She pointed her hands behind her, and the bursts of fire acted like two booster rockets.

Two seconds after I had October wrapped in my arms, Juanita had both of us wrapped in hers.

"Gotcha." She crossed her hands in front of us with her

palms down and let loose her fire. We became a streaking fireball plummeting toward the ground. The flames shot out in front of us, slowing our descent.

But only a little. Not enough to save us.

I was responsible. I had been willing to make the sacrifice, but I didn't want to hurt Juanita. I never wanted to hurt her.

"Juanita!" I heard the anger in my own voice. "What have you done? You should have stayed where it was safe."

Juanita had to yell over the roar of her own flames.

"I am your friend, Rafter Bailey. And I'm glad you're mine."

We continued our plunge toward the hard asphalt of 17th Street.

34

I NEED YOUR HELP

It took Benny a full three seconds to get off the cable and into the adjacent building. It was painfully slow, but luckily, once his feet hit the ground, Benny was anything but slow.

It had taken him three seconds to get into the building, but only another three seconds to get out of it. He raced down the stairs at lightning speed.

The front doors of the building were glass. Eyewitnesses said they simply exploded when he ran through them.

Firefighters and police covered the street below the Baylor. When they saw October sliding across the buildings on a cable, they'd pulled out a jump net, hoping to be able to catch anybody who fell.

Of course they were in the wrong place. They'd been

under October, and with me jumping and hitting him, we were now on a different path.

The good news was that with Juanita's fireball, it was easy for Benny to see where we would land.

A jump net is a heavy piece of equipment, but with his supersuit, Benny could handle it alone. He raced to the firefighters, yanked it out of their hands, and then ran to where he saw we were going to land.

The firefighters were too far away to help. Worse, the street had been cleared by the police. There was no one left to help.

Except for Monroe.

Monroe Johnson. The ankle biter.

When he had discovered that Juanita had been captured, he'd got it in his head that the three retired superheroes from the senior center could help. They knew Juanita. They knew how to save the day. To his young mind, it made total sense.

He and his babysitter had taken the bus, retrieved the three women, and led them back to the Baylor.

They didn't know how to get to the thirteenth floor. They missed Rodney being called upstairs, and eventually they wandered back outside. They were pushed to the side by the police, but had stayed close in case they could help out in any way.

That's where they were when Merry spotted the fireball

in the sky and Benny appeared, dressed in a supersuit and carrying a jump net.

"Please," Benny said. "My brother is falling. I need your help."

I wouldn't have blamed them if they had turned and run. Benny had said his brother was falling, but we looked more like a blazing meteor hurling out of the sky.

When Rodney had triggered the device, all of them had gotten their powers back. Judith, the one with the walker, had lightning. Merry could shrink herself. Barbara could shoot water from her hands. Nothing fancy. Just classic superpowers.

None of them used their powers, though. Sometimes you don't need powers to be super.

Merry tossed her walker to the side and grabbed the net. Monroe was too short, but he grabbed onto Merry's legs and helped steady her.

The women from the senior center, their bathrobes whipping around them in the wind, stepped forward, grabbed the jump net, and held it toward the stars.

35

I'LL KNIT THEM FIRST THING TOMORROW

Juanita and I slammed into the net. The force of our fall sent us to the pavement, along with the women, in a heap of arms, legs, and supersuits. The smell of singed cloth and hair was strong in my nostrils.

I untangled myself from the mess and leaped to my feet, surprised that I could stand at all. Surprised I was still conscious.

I began helping our heroes to their feet, thanking them and making sure they were okay. October Jones was somewhere under this pile of bodies and I didn't know what he might try next.

As it happened, October Jones had a broken collarbone

and a sprained ankle. He was none too happy, but he couldn't do much about it. He lay on his back and cursed and groaned. I tried to help him up but he only snarled.

Dad landed next to us. More superheroes arrived after him. Four of them held October to the ground, and another one went to find the police.

I breathed a sigh of relief, and let them take charge.

I found Benny on his hands and knees. His head was hanging down, and at first I thought he was hurt. I got down and put my arm around him.

"You okay?" I asked.

He nodded.

"You sure? There are ambulances. I could get somebody to check you out."

Benny turned his head so he was looking right at me. "I did it for real this time, didn't I? I did something important. I'm not a nobody."

This time I did hug Benny. I knew this was important to him, so I said my next words carefully. "You are somebody important, Benny. And today, you did a great thing."

Benny sat back on his legs, and smiled. Then he fell onto his back and started laughing.

Juanita was already on her feet, checking to make sure the women from the senior center were okay.

I heard on the radio that Grandpa had found Thimon hiding in the shed on the roof.

We'd done it. Not just me. Not just the three of us. All of us. In big ways and little ways, we'd fought the bad guys.

We'd beaten them, and we'd won.

✳

The night blurred together. In real life you don't just save the day and fly off into the sunset.

The Joneses were all gathered up and the police started taking statements. People who had come out of their hotel rooms or wandered in from around the city were sent back to their rooms and homes. Reporters and TV crews came, and suddenly a lot of superheroes were pushing, trying to get in front of the camera.

Slowly, bit by bit, the police and firefighters got things under control.

At one point, Grandpa came over to Benny and me and whacked us both on the back. "I'm mighty proud of you boys," he said. "Mighty proud."

That made me smile, and put a grin on Benny's face that would be there even after he fell asleep in the back of the Mitsubishi later.

I said good-bye to Judith, Barbara, and Merry before Dirk took them home.

"You won't forget?" Benny asked Merry.

"I'll knit them first thing tomorrow," Merry replied. "And I'll send them to you in the mail."

Benny saw my questioning look. "She's going to make

me some anti-chafing pads. I'm really itching in a few of my nether regions."

Just before dawn I found a parking meter, sat down on the cement, and leaned against it. I was half-asleep when Juanita came over to say good-bye. She was yawning, but looked happy.

"Hi, Rafter."

"Hi, Juanita." Before I could get to my feet, Juanita slumped down next to me on the sidewalk. She leaned against the parking meter on the other side.

I couldn't see her face, but I could hear her breathing. Her head must have been just a few inches from mine.

We sat there for a good ten minutes, neither of us saying a word. The silence was comfortable, like a heavy blanket and sunlight on a winter's afternoon.

A warm silence between friends.

After a time, the Roylance's Tacos van pulled up to the curb. Juanita stood up.

"'Bye, Rafter."

"'Bye, Juanita."

Juanita got in the van, and the van drove away.

The sun had just pushed above the horizon when Dad and Mom were ready to leave. Dad had gotten plenty of pictures for his scrapbook. And he'd spoken to every reporter he could find.

We found Rodney working on a laptop in the hotel.

Benny had fallen asleep next to a plant in the lobby. Dad carried him to the Mitsubishi and Benny never woke up— that proud, happy grin plastered on his face.

The engine revved to life, and my eyelids got heavy as the car rocked me gently.

Sleep fell over me. My thoughts began to scatter.

The Johnsons and Baileys . . . superheroes. Today we'd done something big. We'd found the supervillains and we'd beaten them. But there were still many things to do. Big and small. I'd call Juanita as soon as I woke up and we'd plan where to help next.

Maybe in the future I'd get a chance to save the day again. To do something important. I'd be ready if an opportunity came along.

But if I couldn't do something important, then I'd at least do *something*.

Big or small.